Stand My Ground

Dirty Secret Book 2

LYNN HAMMOND

Acknowledgments

I want to thank everyone who has read and corrected my paper. Each person has truly been very helpful.

I cannot express enough thanks to my editor, Monica Bogza of Trusted Accomplice. I was given her information from another author to help me on my new journey of becoming a writer. I am grateful for her friendship, advice, and late nights where we talk about my books. Thank you for your dedication and hard work.

To my family, who has supported me in this decision to start writing. I work a full-time job then come home and write until bedtime. My husband and kids have shown so much support; they even sit on the couch with me while I type.

To Bella Media Management for the premade cover for my book. I am amazed at the perfect result. Thank you, Reggie Deanching with TheStable & Models of RplusMphoto, for the awesome photo of models Jess Birks & Connor Smith.

Thank you to my husband, who also took the time to read and pushed me to go after my dream.

To all my author friends who took time out of their work to help me with mine. You all welcomed me with open arms, and I am so thankful. Thanks, Authors Jordan Leger and Libby. J (Barnfield)

To all my readers who enjoy this book.

About the Author

Lynn Hammond works full-time as an LPN but writes at night. She lives in Rock Hill, South Carolina. She began to write several years after her father's death. She realized life is too short not to do things you love. Lynn also loves to make children tutus, homemade soaps, and wine coasters in her spare time. Every night before bed, she takes time to read. She loves romance, paranormal romance, and erotica. She is a proud mother of three beautiful girls, two beautiful grandbabies, two boxer pups, two lizards, seven ducks, and loves spending time with her husband riding in her father's old Corvette. Lynn writes Contemporary Romance with Suspense and would love to hear from readers.

You can contact her by lynnhammondauthor@gmail.com.

To find out more, please visit her Facebook page at facebook.com/lynnhammond.10888.
Website: lynnhammondauthor.wordpress.com.
Twitter: twitter.com/LynnHam93518439
Instagram: @lynnhammond28

Table of Contents

1

Lindsay

I DROP THE open documents that the damn lawyer has just handed me onto the desk. This is the worst bloody day ever. I find out that not only has my asshole of a father filed for bankruptcy, but he's also run off with some unknown woman.

My mother stands beside me, squeezing my hand in a death grip. "Can you believe it, Lindsay? That your father has left us? It's all Ben's fault. He had to go and try to take Tawney's business away from her, didn't he? He has used all our money, leaving us in debt, so then your dad decides to screw us even more. Now I have no credit to shop. How can we pay for a house? I can't live like this. Oh, I'm getting a little dizzy. I need to sit down."

I feel like the walls are closing in on me. I'm twenty-eight years old with no job, no education, and not a pot to piss in. My father told me when I was younger that rich girls don't work; they are born to look pretty and marry a rich man. I believed him, and now look at what I have become: broke and homeless.

"Miss McDaniel and Mrs. McDaniel, I am so sorry about this. There is nothing I can do. Since the house was gifted to your husband by his mother, you can't live there. He actually didn't have to pay a down payment; it was already paid in full. His debt was from credit cards, all the fancy cars, the other vacation houses, and his company," Charles, our lawyer, says, gathering up the papers that fell on the ground.

I don't see how my dad, the man I looked up to and who said he loved me unconditionally, could just pack up and leave me. If he was having problems with mom, then that was their business, but how can a father just leave their child?

"Charles, do you know of a cheap place where mom and I can stay for a couple days until I can figure out how to find a job?" I take a seat quickly before I fall on the floor. My legs feel like jelly, they are so wobbly.

Don't panic, Lindsay, you've got this. How hard can it be to find a job?

He smiles, turns, and grabs a card off his bookcase. "Yes, ma'am, I do. I have a friend who helps out our society in need. He owns the motel called Safe Bound about two miles from here. It's a little run-down but has all the accessories you will need."

Seriously? There is no way in hell I can sleep in a grimy, filthy motel. "Thank you, Charles, for all your help with everything. As soon as I have the money, I'll pay you your fees." I take the card from him and throw it into my purse.

I snatch up mother's hand, pulling her from Charles's office, down the long hallway, and straight out of the building's glass doors and onto the sidewalk. Taking a much-needed breath—*Fuck my life*—I let go of mom's hand and lean against the side of the building then let out a scream that has been bottled up inside of me since we found out about dad.

Calm down, Lindsay. You can do this. What's meant to be, will be.

I take one more big breath, push off the side of the building, and square my shoulders with pride. I look over to see mom sitting on the side of the curb with her arms wrapped around her legs, rocking back and forth, sobbing. I look to the sky, sending up a silent prayer to whoever will listen for a helping hand. Letting out a deep sigh, I walk over to mom and help her up.

Thirty minutes later, we are stopped in front of what is supposed to be a motel. But to me, it looks like several single-wide trailers mounted together and painted gray with white shutters. The whole area is covered with gravel, and there's not a blade of grass anywhere. There's an old, splintery, death-trap swing chair near the entrance of the place, and the latticework is topped off with fake flowers sitting behind it. It's so hideous and not very classy, but it's not like it's the Marriott hotel.

I pull into one of the many empty parking spaces. A couple of people are standing outside their door, smoking cigarettes and looking right at us. The only nice thing I own now is the BMW I got for my sixteenth birthday, and thank God that was paid off, or it would have been taken away from me too.

"Are you serious?" my mom shouts when she takes a look around. "There is no way in hell I'm staying in this dump. Please, let's find somewhere else to stay. Hey, you know what? Call Tawney. She'll let us stay in the mansion. She's not even living there anymore."

"How many more times do I have to tell you that Cole's friend bought the place, Mom? She doesn't own that place no more." I cut the car off and turn to look at her. "Look, this is just a roof over our heads until we can figure out what to do next, okay?"

We both look over to the motel. Silence fills the car. Mom leans over, wraps her arms around me, and pulls me close. I return the embrace. The anger I have been holding in is gone. I can do this. Mom and I can do this, and she's the only person I can count on right now.

THE AROMAS OF cedarwood and vanilla flood my senses as I step inside. The place is pretty quiet, with an explosion of different varieties of art gracing every inch of the walls. An island bench that would usually be located in a kitchen is strategically placed in the center of the so-called trailer office. The walls are a pale-yellow color, making the room look bigger. Sheer cream curtains at the windows and soft classical music playing in the background try to make the place more cozy.

I grab mother's hand, leading her over to the island bench where I see a bell and a sign that says, "Ring for

Service." Picking it up, I shake it, making a high-pitch peal echo throughout the trailer. I'm really hoping that nobody will answer. It would allow me the excuse I need to hightail it out of here. But as my luck would have it, a small petite Asian woman comes walking out of one of the rooms. She looks about my age, with freckles covering her entire face. She has glossy jet-black hair, and mile-long eyelashes encase her almond-shaped eyes. She's very beautiful.

She walks over, carrying an extremely large box in her arms. She lowers it gently on the counter then turns her attention to me. "Well, hello there. My name is Holly. How can I help you?"

"Hi. Hope we aren't intruding, but Charles sent us over here due to our recent circumstances in losing our family home. My name is Lindsay, and this is my mother, Evelyn."

"Well, nice to meet you, and I will be glad to set you two up in a room." She taps on the computer. "Room twelve at the end of the motel is open. This is actually the largest room we have. Grover only allows large families to occupy it, but it's the last room we have, and he says never turn someone away."

"Thank you so much. I really appreciate you helping us."

Holly hands me the key to our room. "Dinner will be served in an hour. If you take the hall to your left, you will see the dining room. Tonight is the blue-plate special: homemade fried chicken with loaded mashed potatoes."

My stomach rumbles from hunger. Even though I try to stay away from fatty foods to keep my figure, the chicken sounds good right about now.

"That sounds amazing. After we get cleaned up, we will be down." I wave goodbye and turn to leave.

After gathering up our bags of clothes, we make it inside our room. I scan the place, noticing a small couch and a love seat a few feet in front of me. A good size TV sits above an old, brick fireplace. Not very fancy but homey nonetheless.

"Sweetie, I like it. You know, we didn't need that big house anyway. I think this place might be good for us and will bring us closer." Mom wraps her arm around my waist, squeezing me.

I know what she means when she says this. I was always a daddy's girl and followed him everywhere while mom babied Ben. Things are going to change now. Us two women are sticking together, and we are going to fight ourselves back to the top. I'm going to prove to my dad that he didn't bring us down. We are fighters.

2

Grover

THE DOORBELL RINGS, disturbing me out of my afternoon nap in my office. I look up to see Holly walking in with a frown on her face. Looking up at the clock on the wall, it reads six-thirty in the evening. I rub my eyes with the palm of my hands and blink at the time, making sure I'm reading it right.

Yep, six-thirty. Cole is going to kill me for being late for the party and photography for the new line of briefs Tawney just launched. I really wasn't looking forward to modeling, but he guilt-tripped me, so I agreed to do it.

I bring my attention back to Holly, who now stands right in front of me. "Hey, babe. What are you doing here? I asked you to work for a couple more hours since I have this benefit to go to."

"I thought you might need to know that Ben's sister, Lindsay, and mother are at the motel. I tried calling you several times, but I couldn't get a hold of you, so I put them in the last room available. Room twelve."

Why the hell did Cole drag me into his family drama? Tawney, Cole's wife, was Ben's ex, and Lindsay, Ben's sister, was Cole's booty call and is now homeless and out on the street. It's been all over the news how Billionaire McDaniel sold all his stuff and filed for bankruptcy. Lindsay is hot as fuck, don't get me wrong, but she's a pampered princess and clueless as to how life works outside of her ivory tower. She has never worked a real job since her daddy gave her everything she ever wanted. Well, the princess has a rude awakening coming because no guy can live up to her standards.

I take a deep breath and grab my cell. I can't understand why I have to be her babysitter. Plus, she has her mom too, and that woman is high maintenance as well. I bet you a pound of peanuts right now that she is whining and bitching about my homeless shelter I've made into a motel. I'm sure it doesn't meet her elite, toffee-nosed standards.

After several rings, Cole finally picks up. "Man, this better be an emergency of life or death interrupting my lovemaking with my wife."

I grimace. "Like I care about you two horny love birds. Look, your ex and her mother are here at my motel now, needing a place to stay. I told you I would watch her, but I can't be babysitting her. I have a job to do."

"Calm down, Grover. She doesn't know you own the place. Hell, she doesn't even really know we were working together to help Tawney. Let Holly offer her some cleaning jobs around the motel for letting them stay until she can get back on her feet."

Tawney is giggling in the background. Fuck, those two get on my nerves. Who wants to be stuck with just one woman when you can have them all?

"Okay, man. I'll get right on that. I doubt the girl has ever used her hands for menial work before, but I'll ask Holly." I hang up, slamming my phone down on the table.

Holly moves around the desk, pulling her shirt over her head. She is one I like to keep around. She certainly knows just how to please a man. She was raised to do what was told and not give any lip. She sure knows how to suck a man's cock. When she gives me head, my eyes roll in the back of my head.

I pull her against me, cupping her ass with my hands, then lift her onto my lap. She giggles. I weave my hand into her jet-black hair until my fingers are wrapped around in it, and pull it back.

"You want some of this, baby? I need some release from all this tension from work." I lean down, taking a nip at her pebbled nipple poking through her silky bra.

"Fuck yes," she hisses while grinding her heated, covered folds into my crotch.

Okay, too much clothing. I lean back in my chair far enough to pull my shirt over my head. I stand up and lift Holly onto my desk. "Get naked, now."

I fumble with the button on my pants. I tug roughly, and my button goes flying to the floor. Shit! Oh, well, I keep several pairs in my cabinet in case some of my flings drop by for a little *extra* fun.

Holly sits completely naked on my mahogany desk. I trail my finger slowly down between her breasts. I slide my hand around the middle of her back, making her spine arch so her perfect tits push up towards me more. I take her nipple into my mouth and suck. I twirl my tongue around her aureole; Holly gasps. She likes it when I tease these tits of hers.

I slide my palm down her flat stomach to her heated folds. I brush my finger in between her swollen lips, letting it glide slowly up and down, teasing that slick pussy.

"Going to taste that sweet pussy now."

I grab her ass, bringing it to the edge of my desk for better access, and I get to my knees for the perfect height. I lick from back to front, flicking her clit, and her whole body trembles with the sensation. Her long, slender legs wrap around my shoulders, pushing that sweet cunt closer to my tongue. Using two fingers, I spread her lower lips to have better access to the sweet nectar. I put my mouth to her pink inner sanctum and suck, grazing my teeth along as I go. She moans and digs her heels into my back. While I keep sucking on her clit, I push two fingers into her entrance, curving them so I can rub and play with her G-spot. I suck a little harder on her pearl while thrusting my fingers in and out faster, hitting her sweet spot every time. Her thighs start to tremble more as she tightens her hold with her legs around my head, and I know she is getting closer.

She whimpers, and her entire body starts to shake uncontrollably. Her hands grab my head, pushing it closer in between her legs. "Yes, right there, Grover, right there. Oh my god, I'm coming."

I am hard as a fucking rock now. Not wasting any time, I need my dick wet. I pick her up, flipping her over the desk. I don't even give her time to open her legs fully. I position myself and slam right into her. Holly starts pushing her body backwards, making my erection harder. This feels fucking perfect. I pick up the speed, fucking her harder. I feel the tickle of pressure surround my lower back and abdomen, making me ready to release cum inside her. My body starts to jerk and spasm. I do one more deep thrust and explode inside her.

I pull out, reaching down to dispose of the condom, but there is no damn condom. Fuck, how can I be so stupid?

"Holly, go pee in the toilet and get the cum out. I forgot to cover my dick, and I don't need no damn kids." I smack her ass.

"Grover, I already told you I am on the birth control shot and there is no way I can get pregnant." She wraps her arms around my neck and places her lips on mine.

I don't trust no kind of protection at all, and I sure in hell can't believe her. She's always talking about getting married and having children one day. Hate to burst her bubble, but I'm not that guy.

I wash up and put my clothes back on. Holly is sitting at my desk, playing on my phone. I have some top-secret stuff on there that no one should be looking at, so I snatch the phone from her.

"Don't ever scan through my phone again. I do a lot of business on it, and your eyes should not be looking at any of it. Do you understand?"

A pool of tears gathers in her eyes. "I'm sorry, Grover. An alert dinged, and I was just curious, that's all. I will never do it again." She stands up, maneuvering around me toward the door. She turns, "Come by for dinner. It's the blue-plate special tonight, and you need to talk with the young woman that came in this evening about how to make her keep around the motel."

I just nod and watch her sexy ass while she walks out.

3

Lindsay

I SNEAK OUT *of the house to follow Ben. On the beach are so many girls and boys hanging around a fire near the point. My mother calls it the end of the ocean, where lovers go to be romantic. I hide behind a large wooden pole underneath the pier and watch the teens laugh, drink, and dance to music. I can't wait to be old enough to party.*

A couple of hours go by, and I'm exhausted from standing and watching, so I turn around to follow the path I came from. Crap, the tide has come in and is almost near the embankment. I head off at a jog. Water and sand splatters, hitting me all over my gown and face. I hope my parents are not awake when I get home, because I will have a lot of explaining to do.

Arriving at our beach house, the only light showing is from my room that I left on. I march up the wooden steps and reach out quietly to open the door. It opens immediately. Mom is standing there in her robe, arms crossed, tapping her foot. Oh, boy!

"Where have you been, young lady? Ben tells me that you snuck out and he couldn't find you. Why would you sneak out in the middle of the night knowing full well someone could have taken you?"

I can't believe my brother pretended he snuck out to look for me. So instead of him getting in trouble, he is twisting it around on me.

"Mom, I'm sorry. I just wanted to go look at the moon shining down on the ocean. I won't ever do it again."

That night I cried myself to sleep, afraid mom would tell my dad I was a bad girl. But she never told him of it, yet Ben proved to me that he would never have my back. So, from here on out, I need to be a good little girl.

★   ★   ★

"LINDSAY, DID YOU hear what I said?" mom asks, snapping her fingers in front of my face. I blink several times and realize I must have fallen asleep when looking for jobs on the internet.

"No, mom, I didn't. I nodded off. What did you say?"

"I said it's dinner time and I'm hungry. There probably isn't any food left since I've been trying to get you up for thirty minutes now." She turns and flops down on the bed, letting out a big huff of breath.

We head down the hall till we get to a sign that says *dining area*. I take a look around the place. A hot buffet sits in the center of the space, and there is a dessert table too. My mouth waters. I haven't eaten all day. I turn to talk to mom, but she's not behind me. I start scanning the area and see her. She's made her way over to where Holly is standing. They look like they are in deep conversation. I shake my head and go over to find out what my mother is complaining about.

"Holly, I don't see what the problem is. I was just offering the homeless woman a few dollars to make my plate. I didn't mean to offend anyone." My mother's harsh tone lashes out.

I'm so embarrassed. Here I go thinking she was being reasonable about the whole situation, yet now she's trying to pay people to make her meal. She doesn't get that we are broke.

I grab her arm, turning her around to me. I lean in close and hiss, "What the hell are you doing, mom? You can't do that."

"I'm sorry, dear, but I have never made my own plate of food before. I'm embarrassed, to say the least. Come," she whispers in my ear.

I don't respond, but I grab her hand and lead her over to the food bar. The food looks amazing. A variety of vegetables sit in a gray pan. The fried chicken looks absolutely mouthwatering, and so do the loaded mashed potatoes.

I grab two plates and hand one to her. I think she is more embarrassed that she never took the time to do things for herself. She always depended on someone else to do everything for her right down to getting her food. It's all my dad's fault.

I reach over and grab the spoon and put some broccoli on my plate. "Okay, mom. Each pan has a spoon, so whatever you want, just pick it up and put some on your plate, okay?" She mimics everything that I do, but that's okay; we both like the same things anyway.

Warm, savory herbs hit my taste buds. I forgot how good home-cooked meals are. I smile at mom, who throws down her knife and just grabs the fried chicken.

Glancing up, I find a familiar man looking at me. He's standing beside Holly, as she points over at my table. I look away, not wanting to draw attention, but too late. He is already heading this way. Shit.

I watch him walk down the narrow path between tables, making his way towards us. I tap mom's hand. "Hey, mom, the guy who owns this place is walking over here. Do not say anything bad about this place, okay?"

She turns her head, looking in the direction Grover is coming from. "I won't, dear. We need to stay here until either one of us can find something better. I will be on my best behavior," she promises.

If only I could believe her.

4

Grover

I WATCH AS Lindsay squirms in her seat. I don't know why the hell I care so much about her well-being, but I want to make sure she is comfortable here. I talked with Holly, and she is on board with training Lindsay. Once I know she is able to get the hang of the place, I will be letting Holly go.

After passing several people and giving them a wave hello, I head over to Lindsay's table. I stop and pull out a chair in between her and her mother. I take the empty seat and grab the last biscuit on the plate. *Man, this is good,* I think to myself. I haven't eaten since lunch.

"Do you like to take others' food?" Lindsay's mother pops my hand, sending the bread down on the table. "You should be ashamed. We use manners at the table."

I scrunch up my face. Is this woman for real? She acts like this is some fancy restaurant. This is a damn homeless shelter.

"Um..." I say, trying to think before I speak. "Well, Mrs. McDaniel, since I cooked this meal and it's an all you can eat buffet, I figured you wouldn't mind sharing. I will be glad to go get you some more."

Without waiting for either one of their comments, I stand up and head toward the food bar. I go ahead and gather all the desserts, so I can get back on good graces with Lindsay's mother. I decide, why not let her do some work around here too? These two have a rude awakening in the world without butlers, maids, and gardeners.

Placing the plates down in the center of the table, I take one of the biscuits and move it to Mrs. McDaniel's plate. "Here is a nice hot one for you. Oh, and I found some apple butter in the supply closet. It's made by my grandmother."

"Sorry, dear, for slapping your hand. It's how I was raised; you ask before taking something off the table. Lindsay and I are very thankful you let us stay here. How can we repay you? We don't have any money."

"Well, I was hoping you two could help around here. Holly is having trouble getting all the rooms cleaned, kitchen in order, and working the front desk. I really don't trust a lot of folks, but Cole told me you two are good people." I place my elbows on the table top, waiting for a response.

Lindsay starts to laugh. "You think my mother knows how to clean? I had to show her how to make her own plate. My mother has been waited on since she was a child. No offense."

I sigh, "Well, to earn a keep here, you help out. Holly will show you both how to do it. I will have her start out with something really simple." Does she think she's just going to sit on her princess ass and do nothing? This woman is about to open her eyes to a new beginning.

★ ★ ★

ALL THROUGH DINNER, we exchange glances. It's a little awkward, and I feel like a douche. Lindsay's mother decides she feels unwell and heads up to bed.

Lindsay sets down her fork and pushes her plate away.

"I would really appreciate the help," I say.

"I will talk with mom when I go upstairs. She needs to stay busy anyway. I will go see Holly first thing in the morning and get my chore list from her. Is there anything else you need?"

Well, I thought this would turn out differently and she would fight me on it. "Nope, that is all. I will see you tomorrow evening at supper."

I push my chair back and turn to leave, but Lindsay grabs my hand.

"Hey, Grover. Thank you. I really appreciate it." Her entire face lights up.

I smile at her. "See you later, kid."

I know that was a dick move, but I don't like the sexual response of my body had at her touch. I have so many reasons why Lindsay is not what I need. I just want a good lay and someone who is just looking for some fun. Plus, she is Cole's leftover. I know it sounds corny as hell, but when I take a girl to bed, I want her to only see me, not the ex that got away.

After returning home, I sit on the side of my bed with just my boxers on, stalking Lindsay on Facebook.

Scrolling through her photos, I see one of her hugging Tawney, and her face reflects sadness. This is why I guard my heart. Why witness all that pain when you can just play the field and never get hurt?

I close the computer then place it on the nightstand. Ruffling back my covers, I lay down, letting my hand wander beneath my briefs. My rod is hard. I close my eyes and think of the hot blond with curves that drives me insane. Oh yeah, this is the safe route for me. Me and my hand.

5

Lindsay

I UNLOCK THE door after the third time someone bangs on it. The clock that flashes on the TV says five am. I don't even know anyone who gets up at the crack of dawn, but I figure whoever it is really needs me. I open the door, and there stands Holly, smiling.

I rub my eyes to make sure I'm not still dreaming.

"Rise and shine, girl. Grover said to come wake you up to help prepare breakfast then you will follow me around and watch how I do things," she says in a high, chipper voice.

Good Lord, who can be so happy this early in the morning? "Sure, let me go get ready, and I will be right down. The kitchen is through the double doors, right?"

"Yes, and make sure you wear old clothes because you will get flour, grease, and other substances on you. Grover likes to throw food too while prepping, just warning you now."

"Thanks. I'll see you soon," I say, shutting the door.

Walking into the bedroom, I go through my clothes. Everything I own cost a good chunk of change. I ruffle through to the bottom of my suitcase, trying to find the ACDC shirt I stole from Cole's drawer the last time we were together. I sniff it. I can still smell his musky scent lingering on it. I have got to snap out of it. He is gone and is in love with my ex-sister-in-law.

I head to take a shower to do something with this messy hair. I'm sure Holly was just joking about Grover throwing food. He seems like he would be strict in the kitchen while trying to get food ready for everyone.

I step out of the shower, wrap myself up in a towel, then flip my hair tightly into a ball on top of my head. I reach for the shelf to grab a hand towel then rub a large-enough circle on the mirror to clear off and area so I can see to apply some makeup. I notice I have dark puffy areas under my eyes. The stress of all that's been going on has worn me out tremendously. I miss not being able to go get massages each week and my cucumber face mask. I blot some sealer underneath my eyes and brush on some powder base. Looking at myself in the mirror once more, I find that I look a whole lot better.

Mom is spread out in the bed on her stomach, mouth open, and snoring away. I write a note telling her where I went in case she wakes up, but she probably won't since she took one of her sleeping pills last night.

As I reach the double doors, I hear a female giggle. I push open the door, and there are biscuits flying through the air. What the hell? I take a step closer, into the kitchen, but keep a lookout for objects heading my way.

Standing there and watching the scene in front of me, I'm actually shocked at the disastrous state of the kitchen. My mother would have whooped my ass even though we had maids to clean up. I just stand there with my arms folded across my chest, watching Grover and Holly now lip-locking and playing tonsil hockey. I'm sure there's got to be some rule about employees fraternizing with each other.

Grover lifts Holly up onto the kitchen island top. Both his large hands squeeze the globes of her ass. Her hand is moving down towards his crotch. I almost vomit in my mouth at the scene in front of me. Before I can excuse myself, Grover moves away from Holly.

"Hey there, Lindsay, sorry. We were just playing around. I like to have fun in the kitchen." He walks toward me, brushing odd crumbs off his shirt as he goes.

"I can see that. I'm here to help cook and clean, not have fun," I snap, not meaning to be that obvious that what I saw bothered the shit out of me. I mean Grover is sexy as all sin, and his deep voice sends chills down my spine, but my heart is still trying to piece itself back together after the hurt inflicted by Cole.

"Wow, someone is grumpy in the morning. Grover just likes to have a little fun with the staff, but be careful he doesn't get too attached. I wouldn't like to see that." Holly laughs, but it sounds fake.

I get her veiled threat. I take a deep breath and slowly exhale to calm my temper and hold back my caustic remark. "Well, there will be no problem here on my part. I'm here to work, not for pleasure. Plus, who wants to be with a guy who just wants a quick fuck and nothing more? Oh, and, honey, I really wouldn't want your sloppy seconds."

Well, shit, my thoughts actually came out of my mouth. Oh, well, too late to take back now.

"Okay, let's get to work, ladies. We have one hour to get all the food ready and put into the bain-marie to keep hot."

I walk around the island, grabbing the uncooked bacon on the counter, and go to work, placing it in the pan. Them two go back to work also, and no one says a word the whole hour of cooking.

STACKS OF PANCAKES, bacon, sausage, biscuits, gravy, and you-name-it is on the food bar. I'm so proud of myself for helping out. The others in the motel are standing in line, holding their plate with big smiles. I pick up a plate and go to stand in line too.

"Boo!" mom's voice yells from behind me while she grabs my sides.

Before I can stop the reaction, I scream and my plate goes flying up in the air and comes down, making a loud crashing sound. Women and children start to scream from being frighten.

"Oh, so sorry, dear. I didn't mean to scare you. I was just playing."

"It's fine, mom, but I think we both scared everyone else." I smile, reassuring her it's okay.

I feel someone staring at me, and I scan the room. Oh, great, here comes Grover. He's walking across the room, headed right our way. Shoot. I bend down to pick up the broken pieces, and mom starts to help too. All I need right now is to hear his mouth.

6

Grover

B Y THE TIME I finally got the last pot clean, Lindsay has scooted her ass out of the kitchen before I had a chance to even apologize to her. I really should have pushed Holly away from me when she snuck up behind me. But her hands went directly to my cock, and as soon as her lips met my skin and her teeth ran down the side of my neck, I just couldn't resist. She knows that's my kryptonite, my one weakness.

Without even giving a thought to how this could possibly lead Holly on, or the consequences it could entail, I let it go. I should have put a stop to it immediately. When I spotted Lindsay out of the corner of my eye, she stood with her arms crossed over her very large, firm breasts, which made them only look fuller. Both her hands were balled into tight white fists. Her face a mixture of sadness, frustration, and anger.

When I exit the kitchen, I find Lindsay on the other side of the dining hall. I work my way between the tables, heading straight to where she is bending over with that perfectly shaped ass staring right up at me. I clench my teeth and put both my hands in my jean pockets to stop from grabbing those perfect globes. Then I realize she was picking up a shattered plate.

"Hey, what happened? Are you okay?" I ask, concerned.

She stands up so abruptly her hand squeezes the shattered glass she is holding and crimson red lines start to run down her arm, filling her hand.

"Mom scared me. I drop..." she slurs then her eyes roll to the back of her head and she collapses.

I catch her before she hits the floor. I slowly lower her down and pull out a chair to prop her feet up.

My basic instincts of EMS training come in. I grab the cloth lining that hangs from the table, yanking it off. I hear the crashing of glass and metal hit the floor. Hell, I don't care at this moment.

"I need a cup of water, now!" I snap.

"Is she okay, Grover?" Mrs. McDaniel asks, handing me a glass of water.

"She's going to be fine. I think seeing the blood made her woozy and she fainted."

I dip some of the cloth in the glass of water then lightly blot it on her forehead and around her neck. I lean close to her ear, "Hey, baby, can you hear me? You passed out and scared the hell out of me." I turn my attention to her chest, watching it rise and fall. I count: 1, 2, 3, 4... for thirty seconds. Yes, normal range.

Lindsay's eyes snap open, and she tries to push up. I place my hand under her neck to help. I don't want her to get up too fast; that will cause her to get lightheaded again.

"Hey," I whisper.

Everyone is surrounding her now.

"What happened?" Lindsay turns her head from side to side, checking out her surroundings.

Which is normal. She's a little foggy still and trying to figure out why she is on the ground.

"You cut your hand picking up glass, and the sight of blood, I'm guessing, made you queasy then you passed out."

Mrs. McDaniel squats down and places her hand on Lindsay's face. "My darling, you scared the living hell out of me. Luckily, Grover caught you before you hit your head on the ground. He took real good care of you."

Lindsay smiles, "Thank you. Can you help me up?" Her hand lifts up for me to grab.

I put my hand under her arm then lift her till she is standing. She rocks a little but then straightens.

"Okay, let's sit down a few minutes and get some water in you then food."

Lindsay sits in front of me and takes her last bite of bacon. I watch her plump lips move up and down while chewing. I'm mesmerized by how beautiful she is without any makeup on. Most women I have been with look like death knocking on their door when the mask comes off, but not Lindsay. She is pure beauty.

"Hey, Grover. A guy is here to see you," Holly says, walking over to the table.

Who the hell would be asking for me here? All my contacts know this place is off-limits. I nod to Holly in acknowledgment and push away from the table.

"I'll be right back. Don't move until I return. Are we clear?" I look Lindsay in the eye, and she nods her head at me.

A gentleman stands in the foyer, scanning a magazine from the table. He looks up when I clear my throat to grab his attention.

"Grover, I assume? Boss man told me I could find you here." He gives me a sly smile.

Fuck, what don't people get? I work undercover for the FBI with different illegal activities, but one that worries me the most is the illegal smuggling of terrorists into the United States. I have been hacking into some of the computer systems, trying to catch some hidden crypt, but I can't be on there long, or they can trace me. All that work is dangerous, and if they come see me at the motel, they put all these people in danger too.

"Let's take this to my office a block away. I don't discuss work here."

I write a note explaining something came up at work and had to leave, but I'll call and check on Lindsay later. I send Holly a text and head out the door. This must be really important to be interrupted on a Sunday night. I will let it be known that no one is allowed to ever show up at my motel again.

7

Lindsay

I CLOSE THE door to my room, walk over to the couch, and plop down. I should have known better than to look at the blood running off my hand, but the warm sensation soaking my hand drew me to watch.

Pain pulsates where the open wounds are. Gritting my teeth, I prop my bandaged hand up on the armrest. I lean back and close my eyes to try and rid myself of the dizziness. I feel the couch dip beside me, and I crack one eye open to see mom staring down at me with a frown.

"What, mom?" I croak.

"I'm just worried, dear. You almost gave me a heart attack. I felt so helpless. I just thank God Grover was there to swoop in and catch you before you hit your head on the floor."

Shrugging my shoulders at her, I reply, "I really don't think he saved me at all. He just did what any other normal person would have done in that situation."

"Well, this is coming from your mother, and I know what I saw. I'm telling you that when you started to fall, he was quick on his feet and got to you so fast. I think he may have a little crush on you. Did you know, when he had you in his arms, he was stroking your hair and talking so softly to you it was like a caress. Now, to me, that says it's more than just someone catching you as you fall, don't you think?"

Mom grabs one of the decorative pillows and fluffs it before placing it behind my lower back. She grabs the water off the table and hands it to me. When she comes and sits beside me, I immediately take a sip of the cool ambrosia that soothes my dry, irritated throat.

I replay everything that I can remember happening just before I lost consciousness. I think of what my mom has just told me about Grover's response to me passing out. I do vaguely remember him calling me babe. At that moment, I felt at ease. Then this sudden melancholy overcomes me as I realize just how much I miss the touch of a man and the sweet caress of a man's soothing words. I've seriously got to get back into the dating game.

"Well, mom, what I saw this morning in that kitchen just told me exactly what type of man Grover is. He's a man-whore, a player. I will not become some man's notch on their bedpost." I place my glass of water down, pulling my legs back and curling them underneath my butt.

Mom's grin disappears. "Honey, why would people write someone's name on their bed? That's just the stupidest thing I have ever heard."

I erupt into fits of laughter; I can't help it. I double over, holding my stomach from laughing so hard. Only my mom could take something so serious and make it so funny.

AS I LAY on the couch, the cushions sink under my weight, making me restless and I can't get comfortable. I've slept most of the day. I stand up and walk over to the spare chair, grabbing the pastel blue throw that sits folded there. As I pull the blanket from the chair, a piece of crumpled paper falls to the ground. It looks old and discolored. I flatten it out and notice it's an old newspaper clipping. I read the heading, "Drug bust. Authorities tackle meth ring. Joe Aroazo was killed during the raid upon the warehouse which was being used as hideout." There is a photo I just can't make out. I go over to mom's side table and grab her magnifying glass to get a better look. The picture shows a young guy with a tattoo right under his left eye. I get goosebumps from head to toes.

"What in the world are you looking at?" mom asks, walking over to take a look.

"I don't know. This newspaper clipping fell out of the blanket, and it looks pretty old." I place the glass right over the picture of the tattoo, and it appears to be a dollar sign.

I remember in school, Ben would point out the different gangs and what forms of art were connected to each specific gang. This dollar sign means power. He always told me never to speak to one of them. This sort of gang deals with sex trafficking, drugs, and illegal money laundering. Okay, this is not good. Why in the world would this article be here? I put the article back in the blanket and fold it just the way it was.

"Mom, do not mess with this blanket. I'm going to ask Grover about this in the morning." I lay it back on the chair. "Let's get some sleep. We've got another big day tomorrow."

THE COVERS ARE ice cold and feel like a big freezer; I shiver. I lay there, getting comfortable with the air conditioner set to sixty degrees because of mom's hot flashes. One minute she's sweating, and the next she's freezing. Ugh! I pull the comforter up to my neck. *This shit is for the birds.*

8

Grover

DAMN IT, SERGEANT Filo knows better than to ever come to the safe house. But apparently, one of the most powerful drug lords, Fernando Aroazo, has found out that there was a snitch, an undercover operative, working within his organization. He also put a hit out on my partner Sadi. She's been working on this case for the past several years now. When I shot Joe during a previous bust, Fernando blamed his son's death on her since she was his girlfriend.

"Remember what I said, Grover. Lie low for a little while, and don't surf the bloody internet," the sergeant says. He stands and hands me a cream manila folder. "Look through this. Pay close attention to all the photos of the gang members. I'll be in touch with you soon."

I clench my jaw tight and narrow my eyes. "You know I don't like to be told what to do. Make sure Sadi has twenty-four-hours surveillance. A guy like Fernando doesn't care who he kills, even if they are innocent."

The sergeant shakes his head and walks away.

I need to make sure I call my tech guys in the morning to install a camera system throughout the motel, and I'll just use the extra room in my business to live, just to be on the safe side.

I lock up the office and head to the shower. I decided not to get a place of my own. I roam into the bathroom, grab a towel from underneath the cabinet, quickly strip out of my clothes, and go turn the water on.

The hot water feels so good on my back. I stretch my arms above my head to reach the showerhead and turn it to the waterfall stream. I grab for my sandalwood bodywash and place some onto the loofah.

A short while later, I am showered and dressed in pajamas. I call Lindsay on her room's phone to make sure that she's okay, but her mom says she already went to sleep. I want to head over and just check on her to make sure she doesn't have a concussion, but Mrs. McDaniel promises me she will check on her every two hours.

I walk down the hall and enter the breakroom where I have all the essentials a kitchen needs, except with a few more perks such as a drink machine and a snack machine. Tonight, I think I will splurge and eat a honey bun with Doritos. I try to keep in shape and as fit as I can since my whole family is obese, but I am allowed a cheat day.

I head back to my office to watch a movie and eat the junk food I got. Tomorrow will be here soon enough. I am looking forward to seeing Lindsay again. I like her spunk, and she's so enigmatic. When I had her in my arms, cradling her close to me on the floor earlier, my heart pounded in my chest; I could hear the thump in my ears.

When I actually really looked at her, she took my breath away. She was absolutely beautiful. Her hair smelled like honey almond, soft and lustrous. I found myself leaning down to inhale the aroma of her. When I turned to see if she was all right, her eyes were closed, so I hovered over her face, memorizing every curve and line, and I notice a small speck of freckles dotting her nose. All I wanted to do was just crash my lips to hers to see how sweet she really tastes. I really wanted to feel how soft those luxurious lips really were.

I shake my head to get the thoughts out, but I have decided that I want to get to know her more even if it's just as friends for now. She seemed to catch on fast in the kitchen, and her mom mentioned she was also learning to do some chores in the morning. If Lindsay can run this place, then Holly can be out of the way. I think I can maybe see where this attraction goes with Lindsay. I will have to man up and tell her that I don't normally do relationships but I'm willing to be monogamous this time.

9

Lindsay

THE NEXT FEW days fly by quickly, and I have really caught on pretty swiftly on how things are done around here. Holly has been really standoffish, and I'm not sure if it's because I caught her and Grover together or the fact that he's just told her he had to let her go. Today was her last day, and all she has done is sit at a desk, giving me the evil eye and snide, smartass comments for most of the day.

I have managed to get the foyer, living area, and kitchen done in two hours all by myself. Quite the accomplishment, really. Mom said she was going to help Grover prep dinner. My mother has really been amazing with the dramatic change in her life. She is no longer bickering about every little thing; she just steps in and helps where it's needed. Things are really looking up for us now; it's a huge weight off my shoulders.

Finally around two o'clock, I'm able to get everything done and head to the kitchen to let mom know I'm heading up to our room to take a shower. The grime of all the sweat plus dirt from a day's work has me feeling gross and gritty.

Grover had to leave. He got a call saying there was some kind of emergency at work. I'm relieved that he's gone, because he has been hanging around here way too much lately, popping up out of nowhere and following me around, being nice. It's unnerving, to say the least.

I remember Grover bending down to lift me up as if I weighed absolutely nothing, so I could get the dust off the light fixtures earlier. His large, strong hands engulfed my waist. I was startled at first but then a little aroused with his mouth so close to my inner thigh. Somehow, he got me on his shoulders and walked me around the place like I was a feather. I'm not a big girl, but he acted like it was nothing, and sitting upon his masculine, broad shoulders, feeling his muscles ripple beneath me, made me even more aroused than I wanted to be. Once I was done dusting, he lowered me down to the ground. We both stood there, so close that if one of us were to lean in any closer, our lips could touch.

I could feel the heat on my face from blushing. My body was tingling all over because of how his hot skin felt against mine. I haven't felt like this since Cole, and it scares the ever-living shit out of me. My heart can't take another break, and Grover sure as hell is the type to stomp all over it.

I groan as the hot water hits my aching muscles. The humidity increases as steam thickens in the air, opening my senses, and I can smell my own arousal. I grab for the body gel, squeezing some in the palm of my hand and lathering its silken foam all over my body. I look out the curtain, listening for any sound to indicate that my mother might be in the room; there's nothing but silence.

I lower myself down into the tub and hit the button to change the water pressure to full blast. Sliding all the way up to the tap, I lay down on the cool, slick porcelain and place both legs up on the wall, my pussy bare as the water then pounds down, hitting my clit. Damn, that feels good. The direct hit from the pressure on my clit sends a tingling down my legs to my toes. I lift up on my elbows and start circling my hips to get more stimulation.

"Mmm. Oh my God. Fuck yeah!"

I start bucking up to the water faster, and I close my eyes, pretending that Grover is on top of me, fucking me senseless. My body starts to quiver, and I feel like I'm floating in the clouds.

I get the odd sensation that I'm not by myself, and I look up suddenly. *Shit!* Grover is standing in the bathroom with his hands covering his eyes. I push with my feet to get out from under the faucet. I'm so embarrassed. I grab the towel beside the tub to cover up quickly.

"Grover, what the fucking hell? Why the hell are you here, in my bathroom?"

With his hands still covering his eyes, he moves closer. I can't even think straight. I sit frozen, watching him walk right over to me. My heart begins to pound.

"I was knocking on the door when I heard, um... you scream. So, I busted down the door, thinking something happened. I didn't know you would be asleep in the tub."

I clear my throat, "Well, I am safe, so you can leave, and if you'll excuse me…"

I stand up, lifting one leg over the edge, but I slip and stumble into Grover, which leads to both of us tumbling down on the ground. He grunts when my knee accidentally hits him in his family jewels.

I can't help but giggle. "I'm so sorry. Are you okay?" I use one of my Pilates moves to stand up.

Cool air hits my body. Well, hell, I'm stark naked, hovering over Grover. I'm not sure if I want to laugh or cry. At this moment, when I look down at him to apologize, he is looking at me with hunger in his eyes and in complete fascination.

I feel his warm hand on my calf as he sits up. He slowly moves his hand higher, towards my thigh, bringing my attention right to where his hand now lies on my scar.

I remember the day so clearly when I showed up at Cole's house to tell him I loved him and that I was pregnant. That day I found out he was sleeping with my soon-to-be-ex sister-in-law. I left there so upset I flew home, grabbed dad's old straight razor, and started cutting myself. From the stress, I miscarried our baby at eight weeks pregnant.

I push his hand away, but he captures mine into his and brings me down to the ground. He flips me over and straddles me. *Nothing. Silence.* He's looking right at me like he can see into my soul, but if he could see all the damage I carry, he would jump up and run as far as he could away from me.

"Fuck it!" he says.

Before I know what is happening, his lips crash down onto mine.

Damn it! My arousal between my legs is going to be the death of me. I'm not sure why Grover turns me on, but maybe just one time will take the ache away. It has been almost a year since I have been with anyone.

10

Grover

I KNOCK ON Lindsay's door, but Mrs. McDaniel catches me before she goes into the kitchen, and asks if I can get Lindsay to bring down their clothes to wash. I'm just about to knock again when I hear a scream inside Lindsay's room.

I kick the door open and rush to where the noise came from. I can't believe my eyes. Lindsay is lying naked in the bathtub with her pussy bare underneath the faucet. I have seen some hot shit in my life with women getting off, but picturing her fucking the water turns me on. Her mouth is slightly open; her eyes are closed; and her hair is waved over both shoulders. She looks stunning and gorgeous, and I just want to crawl right in with her and tease those beautiful pink nipples.

God, she looks stunning, and the blush on her face has my dick hard as a rock.

Lindsay moves, turning her head my way, and I rush to cover my eyes. I don't want to be caught ogling her body like a stalker. Before I can clear my throat, she pushes up and stands, grabbing her towel. Her foot slips on the fluffy rug, causing her to lose balance and fall forward. I grab her instinctively, causing us both to fall, and her knee rams into me.

The pain radiates from my cock to my balls. I close my eyes and take a good deep breath to try to block it out, but Lindsay giggles. I'm not sure why she thinks this is funny. Maybe I should pinch her nipple and cause her pain too, but when I open my eyes, she is in some kind of sexy pose, stark naked.

Fuck it. I've got to taste her. I grab her calf, stop her from moving, and bring her down to me. My finger brushes against a deep scar on her inner thigh. This is not a razor nick or a scratch; this is deeper. I look up at her, and I can see the sadness in her eyes. She did this to herself.

Lindsay wiggles to move, but I slam my lips down on hers to take her mind off her sorrows. I want to take all the pain away that she's ever had to endure.

I deepen the kiss. She opens her mouth slightly, letting my tongue slip into hers, allowing mine to play the erotic dance I've imagined so many times since I've met her. She moans out loud. I pull her closer to me, wrapping my arms around her and holding her closer.

Our hands start to explore each other's bodies. Lindsay pulls away but starts to kiss my jaw and up to my earlobes, sucking one in her mouth and twirling her tongue around it. Fuck, she nibbles on it, sending ripples of electricity through my body.

"Oh, good God, your body is like an Adonis, Grover," she whispers.

She slides her hands under my shirt, pushing it up my chest and sliding it off. The next thing I know, she is kissing down my chest and her nails gently draw down, following those sinful lips.

I've always wondered how this felt when I watched porn, and at this very moment, it's turning me on like you wouldn't believe.

Lindsay traces her nimble fingers along the front of my jeans. My body reflexively twitches under her masterful touch.

"Damn, baby, you have no idea how good that feels." I say in a hushed tone.

She glances up at me with a seductive smile on her face and slowly unbuttons my jeans then slides my zipper down. My cock springs free, waiting for her attention. I like to go commando; it's convenient. It helps my buddy breathe.

Lindsay's fingers curl around my huge, throbbing cock, then she opens her mouth and wraps her lips around it.

"Holy fuuuck!"

Her tongue starts to swirl around my swollen head, and then she takes the whole thing into her mouth. I raise my hips to sink my cock farther in. She lets out a moan, grabs my base, and starts moving up and down while sucking me.

My body starts to tingle, and I don't think I'm going to last much longer with her perfect, plump lips wrapped around my cock. With a growl, I reach down for her arms and haul her up along my body. I nip at her wet, supple lips with my teeth.

"You can finish this another time, sweetheart. I've got to feel your lovely, tight pussy on my dick."

I rise and kiss her passionately. I wrap my hand behind her head, pulling her closer. This is so new to me. I crave her like a thirsty man in the desert, and it scares the hell out of me. I start losing control because of her sweet, slow torture. Her teasing my tongue is like a slow, erotic dance.

"Fuck me, Grover," she whispers, breathless.

"Okay, baby, roll over for me. I want to look at that glorious ass of yours while I take you from behind," I groan when I look down and see she's biting her lip, leaving indentations from her teeth.

Damn, she is sexy as hell.

Lindsay's sweet pussy glistens from her arousal while she's perfectly bent over on all four on the floor. I slide my hand along the crease of her ass, pushing one finger in between her lower lips. I place small kisses along each perfectly rounded ass cheek while I work my second finger into her moist heat.

"Please," she whimpers.

I slowly lick and blow on her, and she pushes her ass to my face. I'm losing all my self-control from teasing her sweet, tender pussy.

"Okay, baby, be ready for the ride of your life." I smack her ass a little harder.

"Mmmm," she moans.

"You like that, huh?" I roll on the condom, grab both hips, and slowly enter her.

I let her adjust to my large cock just for a second then I start moving in and out till I am delving into a deep mind-blowing rhythm. Lindsay is rocking back, trying to swallow my dick inside her hard. Not many women are able to take my size. But she feels like pure magic that is built especially for me while she takes whatever I'm giving her. I angle my body and start thrusting, hitting her G-spot perfectly. I pull out just till the tip of my cock is at the rim of her pussy then I slam myself into her as I squeeze her ass cheeks.

"Fuck, Grover. I'm about to cum. Don't stop."

I thrust into her faster and harder.

"Oh, my God! Yes...Yes..."

"Yeah, baby, feels so fucking good." With a guttural groan from deep in my chest, I cum into the condom.

I fall to the side, taking her with me. We lay there for a few minutes, listening to our heavy breathing.

"Well, that was amazing. I hope you're up for round two," I say.

Lindsay laughs, and her body shakes, causing big-man-down-there to become aroused again.

11

Lindsay

I DIDN'T KNOW sex could be so good. I figured Cole was the only one that could turn me on, but Grover sure had my body go up in glorious flames. We both get dressed and awkwardly walk into the living room. I jump when I see mom sitting in the chair, crocheting.

Shit. Shit. Shit.

"I guess you two dears made up. I could hear you both outside the door, knocking boots, and some of the other residents in the hall heard too," mom says, smiling while she glances up at us.

I'm so embarrassed. I look back at Grover to see his reaction, and he is silently laughing.

I pop him on his stomach. "You ass. It's not funny. Now everyone in this whole stinking building knows."

"So, what? I bet this was the best thing they've heard in a really long time. I sure enjoyed it."

Damn if he is not right, but to say that kind of shit in front of my mom? I curse under my breath while walking to the couch to sit down.

"Well, since you two are done locking lips. Can you both take down the clothes to put in the washer? Oh, and whatever got dirty in the bathroom too."

"Yes, Ma'am." Grover walks right into the room and grabs both laundry baskets full of clothes and carries them to the door. "All right, I will start the clothes. Lindsay, will you do the honors of opening the door for me, sweet cheeks?"

He is such a cute smartass. I think I might persuade him to be friends with benefits for a while until I'm back on my feet. A little change will do me a world of good.

THE LAUNDRY ROOM feels like a sauna. We have done two loads already, and we're on the last one now. Grover reaches in the washing machine to grab some clothes when one of my thongs fall on the ground.

I hop down off one of the vacant machines and race over to pick it up, but I'm too late.

"What do we have here, princess?" He reads the front of it that says, "A piece of cake. Bite me."

I scowl at him and rip it from his hand. "Those were a gift, thank you very much."

Cole gave it to me for Valentine's day. I remember he had a little black bag with red hearts all over it. The tissue paper had little red lips all over it. He bought the thong as a funny gift since I would always tell him to bit me when we argued. I would wiggle my ass at him, causing him to growl and bite me on the ass. I think I will just throw them away. I said I need to move on, and this can be where I start.

"Lindsay." Grover's soft voice catches my attention, and he is frowning. "Are you okay? I didn't mean to upset you. I was just joking around."

"You didn't. Cole got me these a couple years ago for Valentine's day. I never got rid of them, but it's time, I think."

Grover looks at me like he doesn't understand why it matters, and I end up telling him about the lost baby. I never told Cole about it. I can't believe I'm telling Grover why it upsets me so much.

Grover reaches for me and wraps his arms tightly around me. "Hey there, it's just a piece of clothing. Don't go throwing away a good pair of drawers. Hell, I will bite you on the ass and make you forget about Cole."

The sound of his laughter causes me to giggle. His hands move down my back then squeeze both round globes of my ass before giving me a hard slap.

"Ah!" I yelp.

"Lindsay," he says, and suddenly he grabs me by the back of the neck, pulls me upright, and slams me against his hard chest.

His lips crush hard against mine, and I gasp. I open my mouth, inviting his tongue to dance with mine. It's setting me on fire more, and I feel more alive than I've ever been. What does this mean? I don't think Grover is ready for any kind of relationship, and it's too soon anyway. Do I even want to trust my heart to another guy again? Hell,

I've seen how he treated Holly. Perhaps I'll just keep fucking him and see how it goes then go from there.

12

Grover

I CAN'T STOP kissing her. When I saw her stare at that thong with tears in her eyes, I knew Cole must have bought them for her. At that moment, I wanted to take the pain away from her. Each time I kiss her, my entire body comes alive.

Lindsay squirms out of my hold, "Grover, what are we doing here? I just want to make sure that we set some boundaries for this so-called good time between us."

What the hell is she talking about? I have never heard a woman want to set boundaries.

"Okay, spill it," I say.

"So, first off, I want lots of sex, but not be used for just that. I want more than friends with benefits: wine and dine, baby. Second, no other companions until one of us decides not to pursue the other anymore. Third, be clear; I want to know the truth even if it will hurt me. I have been burned before, so save us the trouble and tell me beforehand if you decide it is time to move on." Lindsay sighs.

"Well, the answer to all that will be a yes. This is my first time ever letting my guard down for a woman. The only reason I do now is that there is something about you that intrigues me. You have me wanting more and, for once, maybe trusting you. So, I'm all in if you are." I smile.

After I get to know her more, I will share my secret as to why I'm not so trusting, but for now, I will get to know her.

All the clothes are done, and I'm heading back to the office to get some work done. Cole called me while I was sitting on the couch, talking to Lindsay and her mom. I didn't want her to know since he is coming to help me with the hit on Sadi.

I don't really trust a lot of people when hacking into killers, drug dealers, etc. Fernando's guys have been sniffing around, asking questions about Sadi, and from what I have gathered, he has someone working on the inside. There is no way anyone other than the FBI and I know where she is.

"Fuck!" I slam my hands on the steering wheel.

Until this is resolved, I will need to keep my distance from the motel. Once I have wrapped up things on the business side, I will call Lindsay and tell her I'm taking a few days off. Dang, I wanted her in my bed every night. Well, it's not really a place to sleep, just a mattress and a box spring in my office, but to keep her out of harm's way, I'll just give it a few days.

I pull into the drive, and the sergeant is already there, waiting with a couple of officers. The look on their faces tells me something has happened and things are about to get ugly. I stop on the other side of the police car and put the truck in park.

I open the door and stretch my legs on the running board before hopping onto the gravel. Slamming the door, I make my way towards Sergeant Filo. He nods his head to follow him.

We walk to the edge of the woods behind my place. He finally stops and turns around, shaking his head.

"You know that I did everything I could to keep Sadi safe. She is one stubborn woman," he says, scratching his forehead.

My chest is getting tight, and I start taking in some deep breaths. If Fernando hurt her at all, I will kill him with my own hands. I might not be a cop, but I sure did kill a few people in the Army. I really wanted to leave that behind and just do what I went to school for, and that's computer programming. I normally like finding the bad guys through hacking, since they really can never find me that way, but I see this time, my enemy has.

"Grover, I need you to be careful. You are not trained as a cop, so I don't need you going God Almighty on me, thinking you and Cole can handle this. Fernando is on the warpath and will destroy anyone or anything that gets in his way. He's coming for you."

★ ★ ★

"GROVER," COLE'S VOICE carries through the house. "Where the hell are you?"

No one knows about my secret bunker under my office. I had it built so no one could ever find me. With my line of work, I'm threatened all the time. Plus the hidden files of all the cases I have worked on through the years are hidden away in the concrete walls.

I make my way upstairs but take precautions, looking through the peephole to make sure Cole is nowhere around. Good, it's clear. I grab the thick rope, pulling it over to me and locking my feet on it at the end. Then I lift with my arms and climb up towards the door, a good eight feet up from the floor, so if someone ever did find this place, they would have to go through a rope course set up to get down.

I have just sat down when the door creaks open. Cole leans against the frame with his arms crossed. "So, what the fuck is going on, and whose ass do we need to chase now?"

After going over what the sergeant said, we make up a game plan. Fernando is a pretty smart prick and knows how to keep things on the low key, but what he doesn't know is that, soon enough, I will have enough evidence to bury him under the jail.

An hour later, we drive through the bad side of town in a rental car. We both had make-overs to disguise our looks. Our mission is to try to get close to the gangs. I laugh just looking at Cole. This ass chose to color his hair black and have long spikes on top. On the sides, he's got three line parts. The beautician glued on real hair to his face to make his beard. I couldn't help but joke and tell him that was some woman's Brazilian wax leftovers.

"Hey, man, at least I look like Vanilla Ice from the eighties. You look like a freak with those purple contacts in." He slaps the dashboard.

Well, the girl I had put strawberry-blond hair extensions on my head, making my hair long and wavy. She thought the contacts would be a good resemblance of what is in style now. I feel like once I get out of this car, all eyes will be on me, but time will tell.

"Damn, Grover, when Tawney sees this, she is going to have a fit."

Shit, I forgot to text Lindsay.

13

Lindsay

THREE DAYS HAVE passed since I saw Grover. I still have no idea where the relationship stands. We both decided to be monogamous until one of us gets tired and wants to end it, but disappearing wasn't part of the deal. My stomach cramps thinking he used me just for sex and, now that he has gotten it, maybe he is done with me just like with Holly. I take a deep breath, open the oven, and take out the pans of stuffed peppers.

"Hey, sweetie, that smells delicious. Everyone is so excited to try something different for dinner tonight." Mom grabs a pan and follows me out to the dining room.

As everyone files in line for food, I make my way back into the kitchen to get the pitchers of sweet tea. Opening the door, I notice a tall guy hovering over the desserts on the counter. He swipes one finger along the fluffy whip cream.

"Um, excuse me! Hands off my dessert." I slam the door, and he turns around.

"Hellooo, sexy. Sorry, I couldn't help myself. It looks so divine." The guy smiles, and the few teeth he has left are slightly black in the cracks of them.

He walks toward me, stopping a few inches away. I step back some.

"I'm DeWalt, and you must be Lindsay. The residents were bragging about your food, so I came in to introduce myself, but the kitchen was empty. I haven't had a good meal in days. I apologize for touching the food."

He holds his hand out for me to shake. Both hands are dirty with bloody abrasion. I gulp down the ball that rises in my throat. I can see he is probably homeless and can not help it, but that damn pie is going in the trash. There is no telling what kind of germs he transferred over.

I reach out and shake his empty hand. "Well, nice to meet you. We don't have any rooms available, but you're more than welcome to come here every day for breakfast, lunch, and dinner. I can call several other shelters around to see if they have a bed for you."

"Thank you, ma'am. I really appreciate it. I'm just trying to get my head above water right now. Soon I will be able to find me a place."

After dinner, DeWalt helps clean up the kitchen before going on his merry way to find a room for the night. I wish I could help him, but all our rooms are booked, and no way, I'm allowing a stranger to stay in my room.

"All right, time for me to get going. Thank you again, Lindsay, for your help." He reaches out with strong hands to grab and pull me into his arms.

My nose scrunches up against his filthy shirt. I can't really place what that stench is, but it reminds me of a fast-food restaurant dumpster and musky, stagnant rainwater.

"If I were you, I would get your hands off my woman!" Grover roars from a distance.

Emotions well up in my chest. I push off DeWalt, turning to see Grover and Cole standing with both guns aimed at us. Instantly, they lower them. I want to go over and punched them both for scaring the shit out of me, but then I want to cry cause my ex is standing there, and it's been over a year since I've seen him. They both have on a God-awful disguise.

"Grover, this is DeWalt. He is homeless and desperately needed a meal. Since we don't have shelter, a couple blocks down the road, a church had a cot for him. Plus, why the hell did you two have guns pointed right at us?" I say, placing both hands on my hips.

"Good seeing you again, Lindsay," Cole says. "It's been a while. I was just telling Grover here how stubborn you can be. A real smartass as well. By the way, we carry concealed weapons twenty-four-seven, and when we walked in to find some random guy we didn't know grabbing you, we didn't ask questions. So, we pointed the gun actually at him, not you."

Ugh! Men. I point at Cole. "Why are you here?" Then I turn to Grover, giving him a deadly look. "I'm glad you came back to help with this place. We are running low on food, toiletries, and other stuff."

I wanted to say more and ask why he ignored all my text and calls, but I figured I would leave that for a more private time since Cole is standing right here.

I glance over at Cole and notice he is looking at me with concern. I feel a throbbing pain on both my hands from clutching my apron tightly. I don't really comprehend that he is really here, now, in front of me, and how much I've actually really missed him.

I launch myself at him and wrap my arms around his neck. He catches me midair and barks out a deep cackle. "I missed you too, squirt. I'm sorry Tawney and I haven't checked in on you, but she's been having a hard time with this pregnancy."

I tense up in his arms. Fuck, Tawney is pregnant. I unwrap my arms from around his neck and wiggle loose from him. I slide down his body, but I don't feel anything, no zing, no arousal, nothing. I clear my throat and look up at him. "Congratulations! I'm happy for you two."

I turn around, putting my hands on my stomach where my baby with Cole used to be growing inside of me. My heart aches for the child that will never grow up. I feel the dampness of the stream of tears that falls down my cheeks.

Instead of showing too much emotion to either one of them, I briskly exit the kitchen as a feeling of emptiness and hollowness engulfs me. I need to get out of here for a while to clear my head. Seeing Cole again just makes my heart ache and feel depressed. I feel so weak and foolish around him. I always ask myself, why wasn't I ever good enough for him? What's wrong with me? But I never thought I would be able to say that I'm over him. The goosebumps and arousal I once got when I was around Cole are now gone. I realize that we will never be together ever again, but I still love him as a friend, and I don't want to lose that. I no longer need to prove my worth to him, and I now know that I have grown in these past two months here at the motel. I think I'm ready to step up for more responsibilities.

"Lindsay," Cole hollers out behind me.

I take off at a jog toward the parking lot. I grab the spare key from underneath my car, unlock the door, and hop in. I crank it up, put it in reverse, and hit the gas, peeling out backwards and flying out of the parking spot. I hit the brake, shifting the gear to drive, and spin the tires out of the lot. The gravel rocks ding underneath the car.

I roll down the windows once I get on the main road, letting the wind blow my hair everywhere. Strands are slapping me in the face, but I don't care; it feels good. I feel free. I speed up a little more, swerving around a black mustang, passing it then turning my signal on to get back over in front of them. When I pass, a dark, handsome man is leaning out the window to look at me through his dark glasses. I slow down a little, mesmerized at how sexy he looks, but when he pulls his shades halfway down, I get to see those dark chocolate eyes. Oh, yeah, he is fine as fuck. I wink, being a little flirtatious, then zoom up in front of his car.

★ ★ ★

I SIT STRAIGHT up in my chair, making eye contact with the guy interviewing me. I stopped by a convenience store and changed my clothes to one of my nice outfits that I had left in my trunk.

The older gentleman is writing stuff down with each question he asks me. I googled some restaurants and called to see if anyone was hiring. This is my third interview, and if I don't get hired, then I am screwed. I applied for some online classes while waiting on this guy to call me back. I've decided to take some basic math and English for now then some accounting courses.

"Well, Miss McDaniel, I was brought up to give everyone a chance even if they don't have experience. Some of the main dishes can be a little complicated, but since you took some Italian classes in school, I'm going to give you a chance. I want you to train for a week before being on the floor alone." Lark looks up with a stern look.

Such an odd name for an Italian. "Yes, Sir, I really appreciate this. You will not be disappointed."

Lark, my new boss, stands up and reaches out for a handshake. I place my small hand in his. He squeezes and drops it. "I'll see you tomorrow at four p.m. Don't be late."

"Yes, Sir."

I head back to the motel to tell mom the news. Once I get enough money for the first rent, I plan on getting us a two-bedroom apartment. I hope Grover doesn't give me any lip about this. I need to prove to myself I can do this on my own. Plus, I am going to work mornings and lunch, and mom can make dinner. She has really amazed me this past month.

14

Grover

THE KITCHEN IS cleaned, and three hours have passed since Lindsay left. We've been undercover for a few days with little results, and we were just glad to be back and able to take the fake hair and contacts off. We didn't think about what Lindsay would think or feel at seeing us. Cole has tried to call her several times, and I texted her, but not a single word from her.

"Spill it," Cole slaps the countertop, bringing my attention away from the window.

"I have fallen for Lindsay. I told myself over and over again she was just a rich princess, but she has changed, man. I know she is your ex, but I really think she could be the one."

Cole opens his mouth, but no words come out. He sits there just staring at me. Shit, this isn't good. Men always make a pact not to mess around with each other's leftovers, but he chose Tawney over Lindsay. It's not like I went looking for her; he was the one who told me to help her.

"Have you told her what happened to your brother? Why you keep women at arm's length?" He leans against the counter, crossing his arms.

I knew he was going to bring that shit up. "No, I haven't. I wanted to make sure that what we were both doing wasn't just some kind of fling. Lindsay deserves to have a good man, and I want to be that guy. Too much shit is going on right now to really get into it, but I will tell her soon."

Cole nods. "Okay, man. As long as she is happy and you are too, that's all that matters."

"Since we are talking, I really need to get this off my chest. Lindsay should be the one who tells you this, but it is really bugging me."

I have watched too many people in my life make mistakes and get hurt. I think he needs to know the truth about the baby. Lies destroy us.

"You know that day Lindsay showed up on your doorstep and Tawney had just found out your little secret?" I ask. Cole nods.

Shit! Shit! Shit! She is going to kill me for telling him.

"Well, Lindsay and I got on the subject about that day."

"Why would she talk about that day with you? I thought this shit was done with. I chose Tawney."

"Sit." I point to the little two-seat table near the door.

Cole sits down and leans back with his arms crossed. I can tell he is running things around in that brain of his. He is rocking the chair back just a little.

"So, Lindsay talked to me a little about the day she found out about you and Tawney. I could see there was more to it than the shock of you sleeping with her ex-sister-in-law."

"Just tell me what the fuck this is all about. I thought we were all past this shit and moved on, but I keep getting this thrown in my face. So, spill it."

"Okay, here it goes. Lindsay was there to tell you she was pregnant, but she changed her mind. I guess with the stress of everything, she miscarried and lost the baby. She's been depressed ever since."

"Really? Why the hell wouldn't she tell me about this? It was my baby too! This is bullshit." He pushes away from the table abruptly, and the chair flies back, screeching against the tiled floor.

Leaning forward, I carefully slide my chair back. I can tell Cole is ready to fight; his face is red, jaw clenched, and the most intense glare is in his eyes. I have only seen this behavior once, and that was when Lindsay's brother kidnapped Tawney.

"Is this why she started crying and ran off? He runs his hand down his face. I'm such an asshole."

"Look, you didn't know. I think you two should talk, and this will help both of you to move on."

It was time to change the subject.

"How is Tawney's brief line doing? I saw she was going to start a men's swimwear."

"Man, it has skyrocketed. The bottoms feel awesome down below. It's a little tight but loose at the same time, letting your manhood breathe."

I laugh while walking over to my hidden stash of beer in the fridge. I grab two then turn around, dangling one up in the air.

"Let's have a drink," I say walking to the back door.

The fire is blazing in the firepit, and we both prop our feet up, sipping on our beers.

15

Lindsay

WHEN I PULL up at the motel, the sun is just slipping down behind the timbered wilderness. I was hoping everyone would be settled in for the night, but I see a plume of smoke floating upwards into the black night, coming from the open fire. I get out of my car, making my way over to the fire as orange and white flames crackle up into the sky.

I see two male figures facing the blaze. Both of them have a tree branch each, bobbing it in and out of the flames. I get a little closer so I can see. My breath hitches as I see two of the sexiest men alive.

I turn to head back before they can see me. Cole's voice echoes through the night air behind me. Quickly, I bolt down the pathway to the back door. I hear footsteps behind me, so I quicken my pace to a sprint. My ankle twists sideways, and I stumble. I look down; I forgot I had three-inch heels on.

Before I can get my barrings, a large arm wraps around my waist and pulls me tight against a broad chest. I know who it is before I even turn around. Instead of making me weak at the knees, it just makes me sad.

"Let me go, now!" I say, drawing my elbow back to jab him in the stomach.

"What the hell, Lindsay?" He rubs his abs like I injured him.

"Cole, you wouldn't let me go. That's what you get, asshole. Did you forget you are the one who taught me self-defense moves?"

He shakes his head and smiles. "That's right, I did. So proud of you, Lindsay. You think we can go somewhere quiet and talk? There are a few things I would like to talk to you about."

My eyes fill with tears, making it hard to see. I have waited so long to see him again and talk. I tilt my head a little to look around Cole's shoulder at Grover. Even though I don't need to ask permission, I want to make sure Grover is fine with me talking to him.

Grover inclines his head slightly and just smiles at me. "Go talk to him, baby. I'll see you in a little while. I've got to put this fire out." He turns and walks back toward the fire pit.

"Come on," Cole places his hand on the middle of my back, directing me to where he wants to go.

I let him lead me to the back door of the hotel. We continue past the kitchen, down the hall, then into the small office where Grover usually does his computer work.

I glance around, studying the small space. I usually just knock and tell Grover when it's time to eat or just leave his mail in the slot nailed to the door. A lot of pictures hang on a board on the wall beside his desk. I get a little closer to get a glimpse of the guy beside Grover. They both have their arms wrapped around each other's shoulders, doing a thumbs up.

"That is Grover's best friend, who he served in the Army with. Since his death, Grover has not been the same." Cole rubs the back of his neck and looks at me with a frown.

"Oh my God, that's awful. How did he die?" I whisper.

I could tell Grover keeps everyone at a distance. Just knowing he is hurting makes me want to go back out and just wrap my arms around him for comfort.

"Here, take a seat." Cole pulls out the desk chair, and I take a seat. "I think we both need to talk about that day on the porch. I think things didn't get resolved, and it's about time the truth comes out."

"You said everything that day. Tawney was your choice, so there is nothing else to say. I remember your words telling me I was just 'a little fun on the side.'"

At this point, my body is shaking from being pissed. I loved his ass, and he just used me till something better came around. My whole life has been a fucking mess, and my own father chose another woman over his own daughter.

"Look, back then, you were a spoiled little rich girl, and you thought what Lindsay wanted she should get. It was fun at first, but it got old." He pinches his nose and closes his eye, doing some kind of mumbling.

"Yes, Cole, I was a spoiled brat back then. I didn't know any other way to act. But one thing was for sure; I loved you so much. You were the only person that I could count on, and you always made me feel so special." I take a deep breath to calm my nerves. "Was there any time throughout our relationship when you loved me?"

I fumble with my hands nervously since Cole is taking his sweet-ass time to tell me if he ever loved me. What's so hard to speak up? The answer is "yes" or "no." That simple. My heart aches because I have a feeling he never shared the same feelings I did for him. Don't get me wrong, the sex was phenomenal, and he knew just the right moves to tip me over the edge with explosive orgasms.

Cole reaches for my hands, engulfing them with his large ones. He squeezes them, and when I look up at him, he has tears rolling down both cheeks. I swallow hard. I start bouncing my leg with my nerves. Something is really wrong, and I'm afraid to know what it is.

"Why didn't you tell me you were pregnant?"

I'm speechless. How dare Grover tell him my secret? It was not his place. I count 1...2...3...

My attention is brought back to Cole as he's snapping his fingers in my face.

"I wanted to tell you, but so much went on that day, and I just thought it would be best to not say anything at all." I release my hands from his. "I guess you already know I lost the baby. I mourned alone, and I hated you for what you did to me. But I prayed to God to please help me get through this, and he did. I forgive you."

Just getting that off my chest feels good. It feels like a thousand pounds have been lifted.

An hour has passed, and we got a lot of things off our chests. I feel better now, and we both mourn our baby. Cole's phone rings just in time to cut the conversation off. It's Tawney. I get up from the table and cross the room to head back outside to find Grover.

I close the door with my foot, carrying out two beers. I figure, why not celebrate? I should be mad at him for telling Cole, but our talk did us both good, and I'm happy. Plus, I can't wait to tell him about my other job.

16

Grover

I WATCH LINDSAY from a distance as she walks towards me, and my eyes rake over her sexy, athletic physique. I find myself falling for her even harder each day I'm around her. I somehow can't stop thinking about her. I rake the coals of the fire a little, bringing it back to life.

As she gets closer, I see the puffiness of her eyes. She'd been crying. I caused this pain. I just want to wrap her in my arms and protect her from any more hurt she may have to face. I hope after I tell her the reasons behind telling Cole, she will find it in her heart to forgive me.

I really didn't expect to fall for Lindsay, but I feel a very strong connection between us, and I am drawn to her physically.

"Well, there you are, stranger. I thought you would have been done by now," she says, walking right up to me and wrapping her slender arms around my waist.

We both stand under the starlit night with the moonbeams cascading their neon light down upon us. Her chest is pressed against mine, and I can feel my erection pushing against the zipper of my jeans.

She starts rubbing her fingers down the back of my shorts. "I'm not mad at you for telling Cole. It actually feels good to get all the pent-up emotions I have been carrying around for so long off my chest and out of my system."

I kiss the top of her head. "I wouldn't blame you if you did. I don't like secrets, and sometimes that gets my big, fat mouth in trouble."

Lindsay pulls away a little and looks at me with those sexy blue eyes, rolling them at me. "Well, I think you need a little punishment, then." She smirks, tapping my nose.

I chuckle at her remark. I swoop her up into my arms, carrying her towards the little secluded area I found near a stream a mile from the motel.

As I start walking towards the open pathway, I hear the engine of a car crank up and rev. I guess Cole is on his way back to Tawney. He decided to bring her back with him in hopes the girls will get along for a couple of weeks until we get the whereabouts of where Fernando is hiding Sadi. I have called in a favor from some of the officers who I've helped a time or two to watch over the motel. I really don't have anything Fernando would want that he could use as revenge or leverage against me. I'm hoping to keep Lindsay and our little relationship under wraps and just inside the motel for now. I don't know what I would do if something bad were to happen to her.

THE COOL AIR drifts around us the farther I get into the woods. I know we are close. I can hear the rushing sound of water as it hits the rocks. My shoes sink a little from the moss on the ground.

Lindsay's lips caress below my neck then she moves down, sucking harder and making my cock throb.

"Damn, that feels good."

I quicken my steps, turning towards the left through the shrubs till I see the little wooden gazebo I built a few months back to relax and enjoy the open view of the surrounding area.

I follow the solar lights down the gravel pathway. The water is illuminated from the moon shining down through the trees. The frogs croak loudly, echoing all around us, and the scent of pine and jasmine hits my senses all at once as I get up onto the first step.

Lindsay stops kissing my neck, turns around, and glances at what's in front of her. She lets out a loud gasp and withdraws her arms from around my neck instantly.

"This is beautiful. How did you know this was here?" she asks in a low, seductive whisper.

Blowing out a hot breath, I whisper back, "I built this. I wanted a place to go and relax after a long day of work. It relaxes me to listen to the sound of nature around me."

"Well, Mr. Spikes, you are a master of all trades, I see."

I place her neatly and securely on the wooden rail, her feet dangling about a foot from the bench. I reach for the wire hanging on the side of the opening and tap the round button. The floral lights hanging down from the ceiling, adorning it in crystal beads, come to life to reflect shiny lights around like a disco globe. "Hey, what can I say? I'm still a kid at heart."

"Goodness, this is beautiful. Can I just live out here? I see you have a hammock with comfy cushions." She points across from us to where I have set up a little private area to sleep.

I lift her up, placing her down on her feet and grabbing her hand. "Come, let's go take a look."

I can't wait to christen my rope bedding.

"Okay, babe, climb in, and let's see if this can handle our kind of lovemaking."

Lindsay crawls in on her knees, showing off that perfect round ass. I can't resist. I raise my hand and smack her hard against her right ass cheek. The hammock starts rocking. I laugh. "I couldn't resist. It was calling for some attention."

"Well, now you need to kiss it and make it feel better."

"Oh, I intend to. Now lay down on your stomach and lift your butt up, so I can take off your bottoms."

"I can do that." She lowered herself down. I have one knee holding the swing still so she doesn't flip.

After she gets situated, I slide her thong down her long shapely legs. I maneuver my body closer, making sure I'm keeping the knotted swing still, or we both might end up on the floor.

"Okay, baby, I want you to reach out and grab a hold of the columns. We're going to try a new position."

She does what I tell her. She twists her neck around, and my dick throbs knowing she wants to watch.

"First, I want to get a little taste of that sweet ass and pussy you now have on display for me." I run my finger through the crease of her ass.

Lindsay turns back around, laying her head flat on the ropes. I run my tongue in the center of her crack then nip at her ass with my teeth while entering two fingers inside of her.

"Fuck!" She pushes her ass towards me, wanting more.

My little minx likes that. I slap her one more time on her butt cheek with my other hand then I start fucking her harder with my fingers while my tongue plays peek-a-boo with her little asshole. I curve my two fingers upwards to hit that sweet spot. I quicken the pace, and her pussy starts to constrict around my fingers. Her legs begin to shake from the intensity. Then suddenly, she screams my name as her orgasm grips her, sending her into oblivion. I let her ride it out until her body goes limp. I slowly pull my fingers from her tight center. I place a kiss on both globes of her ass.

"Hey, Lindsay, look."

She looks at me with her sexy, hooded eyes. I put both fingers in my mouth, dying to taste her essence. "Tastes just like a Crème Brûlée, but only better."

Heat flares in her eyes as she watches me suck her juices from my fingers. I love the way her arousal smells on me. I groan, thinking about how my dick is going to feel inside her.

"You ready for some little swing sex? I just want you to hold on to the rope, and I will do the rest."

I unzip my shorts, grabbing one rubber out of my back pocket then letting my bottoms fall to the ground. The cool air hits my naked dick, but it's too engorged, hard, and throbbing right now to hide in its shell. I spread both of her legs wider so I can maneuver between them better. Pulling the swing with both hands, I lift it so my dick is front and center, ready to penetrate her sweet, hot pussy.

I push inside her.

Fuuuck, that feels so damn good.

I sink in deeper, stopping for a minute before I explode. When her muscles clamp down around me, I'm ready. I pull out till my tip is at the entrance then I thrust deep back in. I hold her waist and start to pound in and out. The swing is beating my thighs to death, but I don't care, because this is perfect. I'm getting deeper than my dick has ever been inside anyone before due to being oversized, and it feels fucking amazing.

"Damn, baby, I think I just hit your cervix. You feel so fucking good."

"Don't talk, just fuck me," she grinds out through clenched teeth, breathless.

I slide her down more, lifting her hips up just a notch. "Okay, hold on tight." I wrap her long blond hair around my hand, gripping her up so her back would arch. I inch forward till I'm right back at the center and slam right back in.

She tightens around my cock and thrusts her ass back against me. I squeeze my free hand on her hip and start pounding into her once more. Her pussy begins to quiver, and I slam into her again and again.

"Just like that, Grover. Don't stop. I'm about to cum," she pants.

I feel the slickness from her first orgasm coat my dick and then she cries out my name for a second time as her orgasm grips her and sends me over the edge, exploding inside her.

My whole body trembles from the intensity of my own orgasm. I'm drenched in sweat, but that was the best climax. I felt it from my head to my toes.

I slide out of her slowly, making sure the swing doesn't hit my manhood. I pull off the rubber, throwing it down on the floor. Lindsay rolls to her side with a big-ass grin on her face.

"Hey, I think you need to add this swing to my room when I get enough money saved up to move out."

I let go of the swing. "What the fuck do you mean when you move out?"

I don't know what came over me, but it didn't even cross my mind that she eventually needs to move out and get a place of her own. I only allow homeless people one month to stay then it's someone else's turn.

Lindsay sits up in the swing that rocks back and forth, but she maneuvers herself in a sitting position then lowers her feet to the ground. She jumps out, leaning down to grab her bottoms from where I threw them down.

"You're an asshole, and you sure know how to ruin a moment." She huffs, buttoning up her shorts.

I rub my hand over my face. "I'm sorry. You threw me in for a loop when you said moving out."

With both hands on her hips, she says, "Mom and I can't live here forever. I applied for a waitress job, and I got hired right on the spot. I start Monday for training."

I sigh. "So where are you going to be working, if you don't mind me asking?"

Even though I want her to learn responsibility and be an adult, I feel my heart being crushed that she's leaving me.

It's this little Italian restaurant a few miles down the road, called Brivo's.

"Oh, yes, I go there frequently. The Manicotti is to die for."

Lark is from Italy, and when he fell in love with his wife years ago, who went there to study to be a chef, he followed her back here.

"I told him I help you out at the motel. I figured I would still do the breakfast and lunch preparation then head in to work for the night shift. Mom can help out with the rest, if that is okay."

She amazes me every day how far she has come. She's not the snotty, rich girl I once heard about. Cole told me a long time ago how hardheaded she was and how if she didn't get what she wanted, she would pitch a fit, but look at her now; a mature woman.

"Don't get burned out. Let me know if you need some time off. I won't mind."

I watch her as she moves closer to me, placing her hand on the side of my face. "Thank you. Not just for giving us a roof over our heads but for being so kind and helping me learn to be a better person."

Lindsay places a single kiss on my lips. "Come on, lover boy, let's go. Mom is probably searching the grounds as we speak, looking for me."

"Lead the way, baby."

17

Lindsay

I HAVE TO admit, walking through the forest and seeing the special place Grover built and hearing that no one else knows about it, was romantic and unique. I was stunned that he allowed me to see his hidden place. From weeks of getting to know him, I have found that he keeps a lot to himself. I hope he will confide in me and tell me why he hates secrets, and the most important, why he won't let himself get attached to any woman.

We walk down the path we came from earlier but holding hands this time. I get chill bumps anytime Grover touches me, and I like it. I think back to Cole's touch, but it was never intimate; we just banged. The more I ponder it, the more I realize it wasn't even love I was feeling; it was infatuation. All this time I wasted, chasing over someone who really wasn't mine to begin with. Shaking my head, I look out to the dark wilderness, listening to the animals make sounds.

Grover squeezes my hand. "Did you hear that?"

I listen closely, but so many sounds and echoes are all around us. I don't know which one he is referring too.

"Um... a frog?" I guessed.

"Nope, it's a cicada." He points towards a tree that is lit up from the rays of the moon.

"What the fuck is that? Shit, should we run?" I let go of his hand, ready to sprint my ass back home.

He grabs my arm. "No." He laughs. "It's an insect that rubs its wings together to make that humming sound. The males are louder, and sometimes you have to cover your ears."

"Are they harmful?" I ask since I don't know why he thinks telling me about these creatures in the dark is a good idea. Unless he is trying to scare me half to death.

"No, babe. When you hear that droning sound, it's their mating call. The men are inviting the women over to have sex with them." He wiggles his eyebrows at me with a big shit-eating grin on his face.

I turn my head to look back over at the big oak tree. The wind whips around me, making me shiver. I rub my arms.

"All right, let's get back. The temperature has dropped, and it's very damp out. I don't want you to get sick."

He offers me his arm. I wrap mine around his, and we head back to the motel.

When we get back, I have to know why he mentioned those insects.

"Grover, what was the purpose of telling me about the sound the cicadas make?"

"Ah, you caught on." He smiles. "Usually, you can't hear the insects at night or during the day, but since the full moon was shining, the males were ready to get freaky with the women just like what I did with you." He winks as he opens the door for me.

I shake my head and giggle, walking in the back door. Only Grover would think about anything sexual when talking about insects. That man loves sex... a lot.

Grover leads me into his personal office, closing the door behind us. "Take a seat, babe. I have a lot to tell you."

He pulls the chair out for me to sit. Grover walks around his desk, takes a seat himself, and rubs his hand down his face. Whatever he is about to say must be bad. The light that shone in his eyes earlier is no longer there. He opens his drawer and pulls out a large manila envelope and places it down on his desk.

I watch as he pulls out some photos and places them down. It's the same guy that was on his wall. He grabs one, putting it facing me and clears his throat.

"This was my best friend, Tony. We both worked for the Fort Lanur training site in Cybersecurity. We both had to travel a lot to different Army bases to teach cadets in this kind of field."

"Wow, that sounds really interesting. How long did you do this? Where is Tony now?" I'm full of questions.

I always wondered what it would be like to serve. Don't get me wrong, I'm not the girl for the job, but I love learning all that the Army has to offer.

"Well, I still do side jobs for them from my own computer. I don't have to travel anymore. There is a lot I cannot tell you due to confidentiality and it being top secret."

The look he is giving me is serious, so I just wait for him to continue.

"Anyway, we were working on a base about six hours from home. His wife was seven months pregnant and on bed rest. He didn't have a lot of family, so he usually just paid someone to come in to clean and cook for her while we were gone."

Grover sat there, looking at the picture for a few seconds. I didn't know what to say, so I just waited quietly for him to speak again.

"Tony got a call that the baby was in fetal distress, and he needed to come back quick. I had to get two tickets to fly us home that day. He was a blubbering mess."

Crap, this was not sounding good. I move my hand, laying it across his.

Silence.

Grover moves his hand away from mine, reaching for another picture. This one shows Tony's wife lying in the hospital bed with a little baby in her arms.

"So, we get there, and Farrah had already been sent down for surgery. They had to do a C-section. The nurse directed us to the waiting room where the doctor would come out to talk with us once everything was done. We headed down the hall to the little room where several other people sat, watching TV. Tony was so nervous but excited as well. He was going to be a dad. I was on cloud nine because I was going to be his or her godfather. About thirty minutes later, a doctor came in asking for Farrah's family. Tony and I stood and walked over, but so did this other guy. The doctor looked at us all like we were crazy. I finally said, 'Dr. Garcia, Farrah is Tony's wife, and we got straight on a flight once we got the call about the baby.' Before Tony could say a word, the jerk beside us tells the doctor he is also Farrah's husband."

I couldn't believe what I was hearing. How could the woman be married to two men? I was getting light-headed just trying to put the whole scenario together.

"Anyway, to make a long story short, the motherfucker was her first husband, and we didn't know it. So, she was separated from him when she met Tony. They got married and moved away. Farrah never mentioned this guy at all. We found out later that she never divorced the first husband, Shaun. That left Tony and Farrah's marriage as void. Before either one of them could go see the baby, they both had to do a DNA test."

Grover slides his chair back and stands up, both fists clenched by his side. He starts to pace, mumbling to himself. I want to get up and just wrap my arms around him and tell him everything is okay, but whatever he has been holding in, needs to come out. Just like it did for me. They say it takes time and you need to give yourself enough time to grieve, but if you hold onto your grief, it weakens you physical and emotionally. I should know, and seeing him broken-hearted is crushing me.

He finally speaks. "The doctor sat down with Tony and Shaun to give them the results. I was not allowed to be in the room since I was not a family member." He kicks the tin trash can across the room, hitting the wall.

The banging noise scares me, and I jump. "Ouch!" I holler. My knee hit underneath the hardwood desk.

Grover is in front of me on his knees, checking out my leg.

"I'm so sorry. I didn't mean to scare you. It's just that talking about what Farrah did, it brings the worst out of me. The test showed the baby was not Tony's."

I can't stand not comforting him. I need him to know I'm here for him. I place my hand on his face, rubbing my thumb along his cheek. He freezes for just a second but takes my hand, placing a kiss on my wrist. Emotions bubble up in my stomach, and it feels like bumblebees buzzing inside.

"You are the first person I have had feelings for, and it scares the shit out of me. I was young when I went into the Army, so it was just a little fling here and there but nothing serious. What Farrah did fucked Tony up severely. She filed for a restraining order against him because she feared for her life and her baby's. I had to go over there to their home to gather all his stuff. Farrah's husband was there and had already thrown his shit out on the porch. Shaun came out when I got the last load in my truck. He had the nerve to tell me that Tony should be glad he doesn't have any baggage anymore. He can be a free man to do whatever he wants to do. I raised my fist and punched him right in the nose. I could hear the crunching of cartilage from my hit. He pushed me off the porch, and we both went rolling into the grass. He got one good punch to the side of my face, but my rage was dying to get out, and I hit him repeatedly until he was unconscious."

I'm sitting here, looking at this man in front of me who's trusting me enough to share this awful secret that he has buried so far down. I can feel the pool of tears well up in my eyes. My lip starts to tremble. I try to think of happy thoughts, but my heart hurts so bad for him. There is a sharp pain in the middle of my chest.

Could I be having a heart attack?

"Hey, are you okay? Okay, baby, I need you to take a deep breath."

I do what he says.

"Okay, count to eight. 1... 2... 3... 4... That's it, breathe out slowly."

We did this a few times until the tightness and pain dissolved.

"I think that is enough for now. You need some rest, and I'll tell you more tomorrow."

I don't want to wait. I want to know why he is so angry.

I thread my fingers through his hair. "Please tell me the rest."

"I will, on one condition." He holds up his pointer at me like I'm a child.

I can't help but smile. "What?"

"If you start to panic again because it's too much, then we end it right then. This is a lot to take in at one time."

I nod. "Okay, I will let you know if I don't feel well."

"I called one of my buddies at the station to let him know what went down. I wanted to know if I needed to come in since I assaulted the asshole. They got a call while I was on the phone with him that someone heard gunshots at four-twenty-one Cummings street. Scott told me to meet him there. I jumped in the truck, rushing home. I had this bad feeling in the pit of my stomach that something was really wrong." Tears flow down his face, and he wipes them with the back of his hand.

I have this gut-wrenching feeling of what he is about to tell me. It will haunt me for the rest of my life. I can't stand seeing a man cry, because usually when they do, it's horrible.

"I got to the yellow tape blocking the whole perimeter. I got out and ran towards some of the other officers. Jetson stepped out on the porch with gloves on. I knew what he was about to say before he even did."

He swallows, and I watch his Adam's apple move up then down. He then clears his throat.

"Tony took his 9mm and shot himself under his chin just in the right place that it went straight out the top of his skull, killing him instantly. He had gunpowder under his fingernails, Jetson said. I wasn't allowed in, since the forensic team were still there, doing their job, searching the place down. Jetson handed me a piece of paper that Tony had left under his wild turkey."

Tears are rolling down his cheeks and hitting my leg. He hasn't moved from the floor. He lays his head on my leg and shakes.

"He told me he was sorry that he ended his life, but his heart was shattered into a million pieces, and nothing or no one could glue them back together. He told me he loved me, and that one day, I would forgive him for being so selfish," Grover whispers but gets choked trying to speak. "I made a promise that day. I would never let a woman crush me like Farrah did him. But you wrecked my promise to myself. Even though I told myself not to fall for you, I stumbled right into your lap. I want to see where this relationship goes, Lindsay."

18

Lindsay

TWO WEEKS LATER, I'm at Brivo's, setting up my tables with clean linens and fresh roses before dinner rush starts.

As I lay the last rose on the tabletop, the door chimes. This tall, well-dressed, and very attractive man walks in, followed by three bald-headed men. They remind me of Mr. Clean of the Magic Eraser commercial from TV, but uglier.

I walk over to the hostess stand, grabbing a few menus. "Good evening, gentlemen, would you mind following me?" I turn, taking them to the horseshoe-shaped table to sit at.

"Thank you, beautiful. Can we get four sweet teas, and whatever the special for tonight's dinner is." The man winks.

This guy is gorgeous. He has a head full of dark black hair, and big blue eyes that shine when the light above hits them. If Grover weren't in the picture, I probably would do a little flirting with him.

I clear that thought right up and go over to the computer to plug in the order. I make the teas and turn to take them, but when I turn around, I almost run into the handsome stranger.

"Sorry." He looks down at my name tag then back up at me with a big grin on his face. "Lindsay, that's a pretty name. May I ask, are you new here?" he says in a husky voice.

I take a step back then nod. "Yes, sir. I started a few weeks ago."

"Are you single?"

"Well, you're not shy, are you?"

"Order up!" Chuck hollers from the kitchen.

"Sir, I've got to go get your order, but to answer your question, I do have a boyfriend." I turn around to head to the kitchen when he slaps my ass hard. "Ouch." I rub it.

I ignore him and continue to the kitchen. I really need this job. I wonder, if I tell Lark what happened, would he fire me? It's not my fault the guy needs to control where he places his hands. This is a workplace, not some strip club. I place the plates onto the tray and head out to give them their food. When I get to the table, Lark is sitting down beside this guy, laughing at whatever he said. I don't miss the way mister-can't-keep-his-hands-to-himself is looking at me when I place the tray down onto the stand.

I ignore him and start with the three baldies. I sit his plate down last. "Enjoy your meal. I will be right back with refills."

"Lindsay, this is Barbara's cousin, Fernando. He comes into town once in a while after a long business trip just to taste her cooking," Lark tells me.

Well, that's just fantastic. No way I can complain about family. "Nice to meet you. I'll be right back." I smile.

My phone buzzes in my apron pocket. I pull it out once I get back to the kitchen.

Grover: *Hey, baby. Your mother and I are on our way there for dinner. She burned the baked spaghetti, and it tastes like shit.*

He makes a laughing-crying emoji afterwards.

I hope this guy doesn't do anything else sexual, because Grover would probably start a fight. These two weeks have been amazing.

Me: *You are so bad. Poor guests must eat burnt spaghetti while you two come here. I'll have your drinks ready. See you soon, handsome.*

Grover: *I'm not that cruel. I ordered pizza for everyone for tonight, so they are happy. I'll see you soon, sexy.*

Shaking my head, I head on back into the kitchen to put their order in.

19

Grover

I ZOOM IN the parallel parking spot on the main road in front of Brivo's. The traffic was horrible, and when I got on the Studson street, there was a roadblock and a parked cop car. I forgot the fair was in town. Shutting off the truck, I get out, walking around to open the door for Mrs. McDaniel.

"Grover, honey, I know you were excited to see my daughter, but I felt like I was in the car with Dale Earnhardt Jr. during one of his NASCAR races. No more driving fast." She wiggles a finger at me.

"Yes, ma'am. Okay, let's go eat some Manicotti," I say, extending my arm out for her to grab.

The place is a madhouse. People are scattered all around the front entrance, waiting to be seated. Barbara, Lark's wife, waves me over. We walk past the full waiting area, who looks at us with evil eyes.

"This place is beautiful, Grover. The floors are cobblestone but smoother. Wow, and look at the perimeter filled with lemon trees! They make you feel like you are in Italy." She covers her mouth in surprise. But the place is amazing. Lark wanted to bring a little piece of Italy back with him, so they decorated it just like the restaurants back home. I don't know how they keep those lemon trees alive, but it sure amazes the hell out of me. They just hang from the walls and ceiling, giving the place a fresh citrus smell.

"There you are, sweetie. Your woman has been looking for you. Lindsay is swamped, so let me take you to your seat. I just had Lark go back to get your food prepared. I didn't want it to be cold."

We follow Barbara down the small pathway to our table in the corner, far in the back. The dangling lights above sparkle in the semi-dark room. Each table has a fresh rose and lit candle. I pass by several tables until I get to where Lindsay is leaning over a table of four guys, refilling their drinks.

Before I can whisper hello, the guy in a business suit smacks her on the butt. I stop walking right beside my girl.

"Hey, baby," I say.

She turns her head around quickly. Her eyes are the size of golf balls.

"What's up, man?" the guy who slapped Lindsay's ass snaps. My head spins to that familiar voice.

"Fuck," I growl.

My blood boils at seeing this motherfucker this close to my woman. He must have a death wish. I wonder if he has Sadi somewhere close by. I will text Cole and the others once I get seated.

I smack the table. "Good seeing you, Fernando. Oh, and by the way, I thought this place was too close for business."

The smirk is gone. His three goons push out of their chairs, ready to pounce me. "Sit back down, now!" Fernando barks out to them.

He knows better than to cause a scene here in Lark's restaurant. If his cousin catches wind of what his actual business is, the whole family would disown him.

Dozens of people have stopped what they were doing to watch the scene around them. I decide to walk away for now. I will just make sure Lindsay gets home okay since he knows she is my woman. That would just be the icing on the cake for revenge for him if he takes Lindsay.

Lindsay looks back and forth from us. "So, you two know each other?"

"Sure do. He has something of mine that I need back, and it better be untouched."

Before I can say more, she turns around with a frown and walks away. I watch her scurry towards the kitchen and throw her drink tray like a Frisbee on the bar.

"I'll be seeing you real soon." Fernando stands up with a smirk. "Oh, and by the way, that's a fine piece of ass you have there."

I tighten my fist, but I know this is not the time or place to beat the living shit out of him, and those three goons are like apes. "If you know what is best for you, you would leave now."

Before Fernando can speak, Lark walks up to the table with his face flushed red. "Is there a problem here? This is a place of business, not a wrestling match. Take this shit somewhere else." He folds his arms and just stares us down.

"No problem, cuz. Food was great, and I just transferred some money into the business account."

"Non portare problemi al mio ristorante, e hai bisogno dei tuoi soldi," Lark says in Italian.

I had to learn a lot of languages in the military, since I was trained to hack into computers. I just listen to them go back and forth, arguing. Finally, Fernando throws his hands up in the air and leaves.

Lark turns and smiles. He doesn't think I know what they said, but I do. I'm glad I know he doesn't associate with Fernando's kind of business, because he would be under watch too.

"Come, your food is getting cold." He waves me toward the booth where Mrs. McDaniel sits in front of her untouched food, narrowing her eyes at me.

Right when I scoot in, she speaks, "You want to tell me what all that was about? Is there something I should have to worry about with my daughter because, Grover, she is all I have left, and I don't want her to get mixed up in whatever you two strong alpha assholes got going on between yourselves."

Wow, I'm impressed. She can stand her ground if needed. Mrs. McDaniel has a backbone.

To ease her worry, I say, "I promise you I will never let anything happen to you or your daughter. Let's eat."

I watch how her rigid shoulders sink down with relief. She smiles, picks up her fork, and takes a bite of her

Manicotti. I do the same. I turn my head, scoping out the area for Lindsay. Our eyes connect from a distance, and what I see tells me she is not happy to see me.

20

Lindsay

COULD THIS NIGHT get any worse? I had two customers complain about the food being cold when arriving at their table. I only made a hundred dollars compared to the three I usually bring home. Grover and I got into an argument in front of my mom when I wanted to know what his deal with Fernando was. Also, the conversation about him having something of Grover's that better be untouched makes me feel like it is a someone, not a thing.

After closing the restaurant, I turn the key to lock the door. I make my way to the dumpster to throw the two bags of trash away. I see two guys sitting on the ground, eating out of the scrap bin for the runaway cats. They both glance up when I start walking their way.

As I get closer, I recognize DeWalt but not the other gentleman. He stands, wiping his hands on his worn-out blue jeans.

"Hey, pretty lady. I didn't know you worked here." He gives me a toothless smile.

I nod. "Yes, been here for a couple weeks now. Didn't I tell you to come by the motel to get food? The door is always open."

I hate to see anyone go without a good meal. "Come on, you two, I will give you a ride with me to the motel, and I'll heat up some left-over pizza from dinner."

DeWalt thanks me, but the other man stays quiet and keeps his head down. The whole way home DeWalt talks my head off on how he has traveled on foot everywhere to find a job, but no one wants to hire someone homeless.

An idea pops in my head. I will discuss this with Grover later, but this would help mom in the kitchen.

"Hey, would you be interested in prepping meals at the hotel? Since I have been busy working at the restaurant, Grover has been more there than at his office. He would pay you."

"That would be great. Do you think I could maybe camp out in the backyard with my tent? I know there wasn't any rooms available last time I was there," he asks.

"That shouldn't be a problem, but I will talk with Grover and make sure he is okay with it."

★   ★   ★

A WEEK LATER, DeWalt has been a lifesaver, helping mom in the kitchen. I've been working lunch and dinner shifts at the restaurant since we have been short-staffed.

Grover has been a little distant since the scene at Brivo's. He tells me a lot is going on at work and that it keeps him busy. He says that's the reason we don't get to see each other that much, but I know something is bothering him.

My phone rings, and I head to the bathroom to talk. Lark has a no-cell phone policy at work, so I take it elsewhere.

I close the bathroom stall. "Hello."

"Hey, Lindsay," Tawney's voice echoes in my ear.

I knew Cole would have told her. I don't need her sympathy for me losing my baby. It really wasn't either of their faults what happened, and I know that. I really have missed talking to her, though.

"Hey." That's all I can say.

"I wanted to let you know that Cole and I are coming home for a couple of weeks. I was hoping we could spend some time together and catch up. I have really missed you." She sounds sincere.

"That sounds great. I sure miss our talks. Where are you two going to stay?" I ask since she sold her Mansion.

"You remember that bed and breakfast right off exit twenty-three? Well, I talked Cole into staying there since he will be working a lot with Grover on some secret crap for work. I figure you and Evelyn could come stay in a room; I'll pay. We can do slumber parties like we used to."

I'm overwhelmed with memories of when Tawney would come over to the house to stay the night. She wasn't there to see me, but when Ben would fall asleep, she would sneak out of his room and knock on my door, ready to head downstairs for junk food and gossip. Evelyn, my mom, would join us with her herbal tea and listen to us talk about those skanks at school.

"That sounds like heaven. I do have a waitressing job now, but I will just pack my work clothes and leave from the Inn." I fight back tears. I really miss having a friend to talk to.

"Okay, I'll see you soon. Tell Evelyn she better pack a lot of her fancy tea." She laughs.

I giggle. Mom is going to be ecstatic to see Tawney again.

I hit the end button on my phone and go back to work. I only have a few more hours left on my shift. My phone vibrates.

Grover: *Let's go watch a movie? We need some alone time.*

Me: *I would love that.*

21

Grover

I REALLY NEED to get my nose out of the computer and go see Lindsay. I know she thinks I'm hiding behind my work since the awkward conversation at the restaurant. She had lots of questions about Fernando and what was so important about what he had that was mine. I hate keeping secrets, but this one is for my job. To keep her safe, she should know as little as possible.

Picking up my phone, I shoot a quick text to Lindsay to see if she wants to go see a movie. I might even try to get to second base when the lights dim down.

After a shower, I head to pick Lindsay up from the motel. To be honest with myself, I want to make sure she is okay after talking with Tawney today. Cole called me once the two girls got off the phone and said that things went well. Lindsay and Evelyn are heading to the Bed and Breakfast for the weekend for a slumber party. I think this will be good for them all.

I notice a black mustang that has pulled out behind me after I left work and is still behind me. I shouldn't be suspicious. It could be someone heading in the same direction but to a different place than where I'm going. I keep my eye on the car as I drive.

Once I get close to the driveway to the motel, I turn my blinker on. I notice the car slows down and idles after I pull in. Whoever this is does not roll down the window, but only sits for a few minutes.

My attention is broken when I hear Lindsay calling my name. I cut the truck off, open the door, and hop out. The mustang spins its tires then drives off.

"Hey, stranger, I sure missed you." She walks up, sliding in front of me and wrapping her arms around my neck.

I crash my lips to hers. We both moan in unison. She fists her hand in the back of my hair while thrusting her tongue into my mouth. A sensual taste of vanilla and cinnamon floods my taste buds, making me wobbly. I grab her ass, lifting her, and she wraps those naked legs around my waist.

Fuck me. No panties. I just found heaven.

I slip my hand farther under her dress, rubbing my finger in the crease of her ass then letting it slide farther down till I find her entrance. It's slick from her wetness. I maneuver her so her back is against the truck door. I need better access to that sweet pussy of hers.

I slip one finger in. She gasps and her breathing gets rapid.

"Tell me what you want?" I let out a growl, my dick stretching tight against my jeans.

Breathless, she says, "Fuck me."

Who am I to argue with that? "Okay, baby, I'm going to lift you so I can open the truck door. I don't want no one seeing that sexy pink pussy of yours."

Lowering her on the leather seat, I pull over the halter top of her dress, letting her breasts pop out. I lower my head to take in her right nipple into my mouth. Her back arches while I'm twisting my tongue around and sucking. She whimpers. I move on to the other nipple, toying with it. She is getting louder with her moans.

I move upwards, placing small raspberry kisses up her chest towards her neck. I use my right hand to pop my button loose then push the jeans down.

Lindsay uses her foot to push the rest of my jeans off then throws them over her head. I'm commando. My dick touches her mound. She slides her hand between us, wrapping her fingers around my cock.

"Lindsay," I moan, my lips crashing against hers.

She places me at her damp entrance. My dick is throbbing; it wants in so bad. I level above her, detaching our lips.

Her gaze glimmers up to mine. She knows what I'm thinking. I slowly enter her.

"Shirt off. I want to feel skin on skin." She slides her hands under my shirt, pulling it over my head and throwing it on the dashboard.

I start moving in and out, making love to her. I don't want it to be fast this time. I want her to feel how much she means to me. This is me giving her everything I have to offer. I love her.

Pushing myself up, I grasp her leg, forcing it straight and letting it relax against my shoulder. At this angle, I can go deeper and hit those pleasure points. I start to pound inside her. Her body is rocking back and forth on the seat. Watching her breasts bounce all over the place makes me fuck her harder.

Lindsay tightens around my dick as she reaches her peak, and that pleasure takes me over with her. It feels like I've been coming forever. When I think I'm done, it's still pouring inside her. I thrust one more time, consumed.

I pull out, and Lindsay's eyes are still closed, but a smile is on her face. She looks so content. I lower my mouth to her ear and whisper, "I love you."

I can't believe I finally said those words. But I have fallen head over heels for this girl in front of me, and I can't wait to spend my life with her.

I'm not sure if I should have said those three words. Maybe it was too soon. Hell, most women beg to hear them.

A few minutes go by, and she still lies there, looking at me with those intense blue eyes. She is biting her lip like she's trying to figure out what to say next. Well, I'm sure as hell not going to wait. I sit up, lean over, and pick up my shirt, pulling it over my head. I find my pants hanging on the steering wheel. I look back over at Lindsay, and this time she is frowning.

22

Lindsay

I'M FROZEN IN place, still naked on the seat. Grover just told me he loves me. I open my mouth to speak, but no words come out. Those words are very powerful, and I'm not sure if I am ready to say that again. I think maybe he's getting lust confused with love.

He snatches for his pants, maneuvering around to put them back on. I roll over to reach my dress when the slam of the truck door startles me. I jump up, throwing the dress over my head and slithering it down. I slide over to the passenger side to get out. I fumble with the door handle, push, and it flies open. I jump down and run down the street.

I do a slight jog to try to catch up to him. He is about a good mile ahead of me. "Grover!" I shriek.

He keeps walking, not even taking a glimpse back at me. I can't believe I am chasing him down a dark, creepy road where reptiles or any other animal can jump out at any moment. I am terrified and on the verge of freaking out. No streetlights are anywhere around.

"I'm sorry if I hurt your feelings. Please stop so we can talk about this," I beg, screaming louder.

He stops and spins around to face me. It is so dark I can just see the silhouette of his body.

"You have no idea how hurt I am right now. You know, with everything I have been through, how hard it was for me to tell you I love you."

"I know and I'm sorry. I do care about you a great deal, but it's a little too soon to say we love each other. I really want to see this relationship grow. You actually opened my heart to the possibility to be able to love again, so just be patient with me." Tears brim my eyes.

Grover starts walking towards me. "That's all you have to say? When you just looked up at me like a deer caught in the headlights, it kind of hurt my manhood." His husky voice echoes in the empty street.

I see beams of light shine on Grover as he is walking towards me and hear the roar of a vehicle suddenly coming up behind me. Whoever is driving is sure not paying attention to the road. They accelerate rapidly, spinning their wheels on the pavement, and rocks ricochet against the body of the car.

I step off the side of the road onto the grass. I notice Grover is running toward me. He keeps yelling for me to run.

"Why are you telling me to run?" I yell back.

A loud screeching sound of tires howling on the asphalt hits my ears, and the smell of burning rubber hits my senses all at the same time. I look over and notice a sleek, shiny black mustang. It looks just like the one that stopped in front of the motel. Before I can run, a guy opens the back door and grabs my arm.

"Help," I cry out.

I elbow him in the gut, but that just pisses him off more. Another guy in the back seat punches me in the face. I hiss with pain. A cloth is put over my nose, and I struggle with everything I have to break free, but darkness sets in.

I WAKE UP with a severe sore throat, and my head feels like someone hit me over the head with a hammer and it's about to explode. I try to move but yelp in pain. I push up to try to sit, but I'm shoved back down by a set of huge hands that are like manacles.

"Stay still, or I will have to make you take another nap," a deep, gruff, man's voice hisses in my ear.

I shift my head around to look at who is talking. The place looks like an abandoned warehouse. Everything has been gutted out. The only things I can see are walls and ceilings.

A scraping metal sound brings my eyes back to the guy in the ski mask. He takes a seat beside me.

The hairs on the back of my neck stand on end when I hear a familiar voice. Fernando is leaning against a rusted pole. He is wearing black denim jeans and a black wife-beater shirt.

The way he is smiling at me does nothing to calm my nerves. It makes things worse. He pushes off the pole and walks slowly towards me. He pulls something out of his pocket; it looks like a blade.

"I was hoping to get to know you a little and maybe ask you on a date, but then I see you're involved with Grover." He stalks to the bed, crawling up my body and sitting on my stomach. He places his large hand around my neck and squeezes, making it almost impossible to breathe. He is choking me.

My throat starts to close, and I can't swallow or breathe. I try to buck him off, but the other guy wraps both his hands around my ankles, holding them still while Fernando puts more pressure on my throat.

Fernando lets go of my neck. He traces his finger down my chest in between my breasts. "Where does Grover keep the evidence?"

As tears run down my face, I shake my head. "I don't know what you're talking about."

Fernando scowls. He lifts the weapon in his hand. It looks like a barber's shaving blade. "See this? I will cut your whole body up until you confess where Grover hides all the information he's got on me."

"I don't know what the hell you are talking about." I focus on the blade.

He leans forward, takes the blade, and nicks my right nipple. It sends a sharp pain across my breast. I yelp. With tears streaming down my face, I close my eyes. I can't watch this anymore.

"I'm going to keep cutting you until you tell me what I want to know." His deep voice rumbles above me.

Fernando starts nicking my skin all over. I scream until I have no voice left. The pain is so severe I start sweating, or maybe it's all the blood. I look him straight in the eyes while he laughs and makes little nicks all over my body. I start to get nauseated. I have to lean over and throw up on the nasty mattress.

"Fuck, she got vomit on me," another guy says from beside me.

I can't open my eyes. They are so heavy. I instantly feel a searing pain in my head. Someone punches me several times on my face until I can't feel anything at all. Then darkness surrounds me and drags me into nothingness.

23

Grover

"HEY, SERGEANT, HE has her." My hand shakes while holding the phone to my ear.

"Okay, calm down. I have half the PD on their way. Do not touch anything."

The phone goes silent.

There is no evidence except the three bald men from the restaurant who were in the car. The windows were tinted, so I didn't really get a good look at the one in the passenger seat, but I bet my money it was Fernando.

I decide to run back to my business and grab the only thing that will save Lindsay. Fernando knows what I have could put him in prison and even give him the death penalty.

"This better be good," Cole says halfway asleep.

It's now midnight. "He's got Lindsay."

I hear mumbles of cussing and ruffling of clothes. A loud tap comes from my earpiece. Damn. I rub my ear.

"You were supposed to protect her. That's why I told you not to get involved with her. He went for your one weakness, and that's the one person you love more than anything. Fuck!" I hear a door slam.

"Look, I have Bear and Clutch roaming now. I put a tracker on her earring, but it's not pulling up, so that means they found it, or she is somewhere with no service. Both guys are trying to get signal while they are out and about to see if it will pick up. I'm heading home for the evidence. If I must, I will hand it over for her. I do love her."

"I know," Cole says. "Okay, it will take me a couple hours to get there. Tawney is already packing our clothes. Oh, and, Grover?"

"Yes." I wait to hear what he is about to say.

"That motherfucker will not be getting shit except a bullet between his eyes." The line goes dead.

I'M SPEEDING WAY over the limit after getting the file and flash drive. I made sure to make a copy just in case. I left Sergeant Filo a voice mail letting him know the whereabouts of where Bear thinks Fernando is hiding her. When I pull the place up on Google Maps, the warehouse looks like it could fall apart at any moment.

I zoom in while waiting on the stoplight to turn green. It appears to be located where the Old Mill hill used to be. A lot of homeless people hang out there for cover.

I toss the cell phone beside me and head towards downtown. I continue down the road until I see the railroad tracks and the bridge they call "Crybaby Bridge." Some old wife's tale about a woman throwing her baby over the bridge since it wouldn't stop crying. They said at night you can hear the baby cry.

The ride over the bridge is very bumpy. The potholes in the road are as big as my F250 truck tires. I keep my eyes straight ahead, watching as the little green signs of roads appear from my headlights. When I see Willowbrook, I turn down the dirt road where Bear and Clutch are hiding.

Both guys are camouflaged in hunting clothes. Their faces are painted green. I knew they would be here when I called these two guys for help. We all stick together. I worry a little about Clutch since he lost his wife during a previous gang job that went wrong and killed innocent people. I just hope in this scenario he's got his shit together. I don't want to lose Lindsay.

I get out of the truck, turn off my lights, and make sure it can't be seen from the main road. I make my way down the road about a half-mile and stop in front of Clutch.

"Hey, man," he says, shaking my hand. "We have scoped the whole perimeter. Fernando has his goons all over the place, but I found a back entrance that we can go through."

"Good. I'm ready to bring that asshole down for good this time."

Bear walks up with folded clothes. "Here, man, put this shit on. We are going in the army way. We are trained to fight the enemies, and that is what that motherfucker is going to get."

I grab them and head towards the nearby trees. I look back at them both. "Thank you both. I know how hard it is for you, Clutch." I turn back, sprinting into the dark woods to change.

24

Lindsay

BOTH MY HANDS are so numb I've lost all feeling in them. My arms ache from being held above my head. The guy in the ski mask hammered a hook in the wall and placed the handcuffs on it. My upper body is lifted, and my ankles are tied with thick, coarse, hemp rope.

"Ah, you're awake," Fernando states when he stands up from his chair.

"Look, I don't know what you expect me to say. Grover is a very secretive man. Hell, I have never been to his business. I don't have anything to do with what's going on between you two," I whisper hoarsely from his choking me.

"So, let me enlighten you a little about your lover. See, Grover and his partner were trying to make it very difficult for me in my line of work. Let's just say that my business isn't your everyday, run-of-the-mill transaction. Then one day, my son brings home this gorgeous woman who is about ten years older than he is. She talks all sophisticated and is very charming with her words. He actually met her at Brivo's where my cousin works."

Silence.

He bellows.

He walks closer and kneels in front of me, holding a knife in his hand again. He runs the sharp tip down the center of my chest then pushes harder, slicing my skin open. Pain immediately emanates through my chest. I close my eyes too exhausted to fight back. The excruciating burning sensation lingers while he continues to slice the flesh down my stomach, stopping right at my pubic area.

"See, Darling, my foolish son started seeing this woman named Sadi. After a couple of weeks, he started getting sloppy at his job. One night, he got distracted by the imprudent woman. He was on a job, and that ended up getting the stupid fool killed. And get this, Grover was the one to end my son's life. Sadi was Grover's partner."

Shit. Grover killed his son. No wonder this guy is out for blood. I'm pretty sure that I will not make it out of here alive.

He presses the knife harder against the puffy part of my pelvis, enough to break the skin. I close my eyes as tears fall down my cheeks. The burning sensation is so severe I start to shake with the pain.

Suddenly, I hear a female voice yelling, and it keeps getting louder until I hear a gunshot ring out. Then absolute silence.

Fernando pushes off the bed quickly, removing the blade. I sigh in relief. I open one eye to peek at my surroundings. Fernando has moved away, wiping his sharp blade on his pants' leg then placing it in his back pocket. The two goons who were watching him torture me go running in the direction of the gunfire.

Fernando looks at me with a wicked grin on his sadistic face, "I'll be back to play with you soon." He turns and heads in the same direction the others went.

I can hear chatter from a distance. I wiggle my hands around in circles, trying to slide the cuffs off. Nothing is budging. I give up and let my body relax against the bed. The slices in my flesh sting when I move around. Heaps of blood start to pool underneath me.

There is a loud booming sound like an explosion. I see gray dust and debris flying around. A hot piece of glowing metal hits the side of the bed. The thing is melting the fabric.

"Someone help. Please help me," I scream.

I hear more chatter then further gunshots go off again in the distance. Sirens pierce in the background. I just wait and hope that they find me before Fernando gets back.

25

Grover

WE JOG DOWN a narrow pathway to the warehouse. It's close to two in the morning, so the air is a little muggy and damp.

A small light shines in the distance where the abandoned building lies. We maneuver our way along the path till we come to a rusty, beat up, metal structure that is perched on just red clay dirt. The whole surrounding area is just barren sand, no grass or weeds at all.

"Look, they have the place surrounded with more men now," Clutch says.

I see at least ten guards holding a gun to their side. "Okay, let's crawl down this hill then try to make a run for it. To be on the safe side, have guns out and ready to fire."

We make a run for it. I motion for Clutch to go to one side of the building, and Bear takes the other. I figured we could split up and eventually meet inside.

I make a run for it. Crunching sounds of the red dirt and stones flinging from under my boots resonate into the night. I get halfway there when gunshots go off inside.

"Shit," I mumble under my breath.

In that instant, Lindsay comes to mind. Did someone shoot her? My chest tightens. I can hear the roaring of my heartbeat in my ears. I pull out my phone, turning on the tracker I have on her. It beeps red. I let out the breath I didn't know I was holding. Thank you, Jesus.

I look back up to where Fernando's men await, but no one is in sight. I scan around and see the guys. I motion with a signal that I've got a trace.

We all head to the same entrance in the back. I edge up first to investigate through the small window on the door. There is nothing inside this place except for old rusty poles. But wait! My eye catches something in the center, like maybe a box spring. I can't be sure until I get in and scope my surroundings.

I duck down into a squatting position and slide the door open quietly. It's already unlocked. The smell of sour piss and body odor hits my senses. I gag, holding my breath and making my way in farther. The guys take opposite directions, holding their noses.

I can't help but laugh a little even in this predicament. We're three grown-ass men who are six foot three, two hundred and eighty pounds, and we're getting nauseated from the smell in here. Hell, we have smelled burned flesh and the metallic smell of blood from bodies before.

The guys are out of sight now. I inch in closer, heading straight towards the object that is laid in the center of the building. In the corner of my eye, a body catches my attention. From the build, it looks to be a woman. I swallow nervously, hoping and praying that is not my girl. I get closer and touch the person. She doesn't move. The brown hair is matted in knots. I get down on my knees, lean over, and check her pulse first.

I sigh with relief. Whoever this is, she is alive. I brush off the hair that is stuck on the side of her face and see it is covered with small nicks. Dried blood is plastered all over. I lean in closer for a better look. The lighting in here sucks, and I can't really see that good.

I freeze. It's Sadi. She has been beaten badly. Her face is black and blue. Both her eyes are swollen. Adrenaline shoots through my body, making me sweat all over. My instinct is to kill this motherfucker right now. But I have another plan in mind. A slow death.

"Holy shit," Bear says through clenched teeth from behind me.

"Did you see Lindsay?"

He shakes his head no.

"I did see a few dead guys laying in a puddle of their own blood. Whoever shot them surely knows what they are doing. Hit them right in between the eyes."

I start raking my brain on who that could be. I know it couldn't be Cole; he was still an hour out.

"All right, stay with her. I'm turning my location on for Sarge and Cole."

I really hate the killing part of the army. You shoot to kill. We are trained to fight till death. Just seeing Sadi's body so beaten, it worries me that Lindsay has been treated the same or maybe worse.

I'm not sure how Clutch is taking this scene. I remember the night like it just happened.

We all went to the Salty Dog to go eat. Bear thought that's where all the women went to get a good hot dog. We laughed our ass off when it was an American cuisine restaurant. We got the call right after our order. Clutch's girlfriend, Marissa, was with us, and there was no time to take her back to the house. Right when we turned on the road the GPS directed us to, two cars pulled out from the dark roads. Guns were fired quickly before we could even react. The bullet hit Marissa in the back of her head, killing her instantly. That night Clutch killed everyone in both cars without batting an eyelash.

A slap to the back of my head has me turning around quickly, ready to aim and fire. Cole is standing there with his finger across his lips, telling me to shush.

"What the fuck, Grover? You can't zone out like that. You are in a warehouse with a ton of Fernando's men ready to kill you instantly."

"Look, I don't have time for your—" Gunshots go off again.

I turn and head toward the gray puff of smoke in the warehouse. Cole lifts his AR.

26

Lindsay

HOLLY IS HERE. She points the gun at Fernando. She fired those shots so quickly at those two guards before they could even aim their guns. This is not your ordinary female. She's been trained to kill.

"Holly," Fernando's voice sounds distraught. "What a lovely surprise. I didn't know you got out."

He takes a step in her direction, slowly reaching in his pocket for the knife.

"I wouldn't do that if I were you. I learned from the best, and killing you would be the highlight of my day." Her voice is firm, not a quiver in the tone. She pins him with a smirk, never letting her finger move from the trigger. "Do you remember that night? Five years ago, when you killed my brother?"

Fernando pulls his hand away from his pocket. He rocks back onto his heels. "Of course, I do. Your brother was a fucking snitch. I lost a billion dollars from that drug bust. His time was up, darling. Just like your uncle's. This is business, and whoever crosses you, family or not, are dead."

Holly stands up straight, anger burning in her eyes. "No, you see. We are loyal when it comes to family. You are just a pathetic wannabe, and it's time you go to hell."

This is so overwhelming to hear. These people do all kinds of illegal stuff. My head is spinning with these two going at it with each other. I fight some more to get the cuffs off, but they are not budging.

Pop. Pop. Pop.

People are screaming, but it sounds so static-y. I push myself up just a little. Two large military-looking dudes stand a few feet from the bed. Their faces are painted. Looks just like out of one of those Mash movies.

Holly comes into view. She walks over with a blanket and covers my body. She starts working on the cuffs right away.

I moan from the slight pain, but then I feel relief. I sit up abruptly, pulling the cover up. My breasts were in full sight from Fernando cutting my clothes. My naked pussy was in full view also. I peek under the cover to see how much damage he did with all the cuts. Dried, clumpy blood covers my chest all the way down between my legs.

"Get the medic now," Holly says in a stern voice.

Where is Grover?

Someone rubs a hand over the side of my face. I know his touch. It's him, but my body won't allow me to turn my head. Darkness sets in.

I AWAKE TO a loud, beeping noise. I still. Memories of what happened flood my mind. I look around the room. I'm in the hospital. I slowly turn my head toward the window ledge. I smile. Grover is laid back with his mouth wide open, snoring.

"Good, you're awake," Holly says quietly, walking in with a big brown teddy bear. I smile at the cute stuffed animal she places beside me.

"Thank you. I love it." I reach to grab it and pain radiates down my fingers. My wrists are bandaged up.

"Be careful. You really did a number on those wrists trying to get out of the cuffs."

I have to ask, "Holly, can I ask you a question?"

"I was wondering when you would get around to your investigation." She laughs. "Grover should have been a lawyer with all the questions he asked me in the warehouse."

"How did you know where I was?"

She takes the empty chair that is against the wall and drags it over to the side of the bed. She takes a seat and leans over closely. "My family is very dangerous back home. I was sworn into secrecy. I can tell you only this much; my uncle runs a risky business back home in Japan."

Okay, maybe I don't want to know. Just seeing the fear in her eyes gives me goosebumps.

I reach for her hand and squeeze it gently. She clears her throat.

"I want to apologize for being such a bitch to you that day. I was using Grover to get close to Fernando. I was worried he would get distracted by you and delay my plans to catch that son of a bitch." She looks straight ahead at Grover then back at me. "I was there, that night Fernando took you. I followed him to the warehouse without a trace. That's one thing I'm very good at, being invisible. They call me the 'ghost girl' back home."

"So, you do exist?" Grover asks. We both jump at the sound of his voice.

"Well, hello to you too, asshole. I sure do, but not for long. I have to get down to some business then I'll disappear again." She flips him the bird.

Okay, the tension in the room is getting heavy. These two are staring at each other with hate in their eyes. You would have never known that a couple of months ago, they were sexual partners.

Grover waits a few seconds before standing and walking towards me. From the slight stiffness of Holly's hand, which I still hold, I assume she's ready to jump at any moment.

"We need to talk. Now! Outside," Grover snaps, turns, and walks to the door, holding it open for Holly to follow him out.

She pulls her hand from mine. I look up at her and she smiles. "It's okay. We will try to fight nicely outside. I have left my number for you attached to the teddy bear's neck bow. You call me if you ever need me." Holly turns and walks out the door.

Grover mouths, "I'll be right back. I love you."

I mouth back, "Ditto." I can't say the words just yet. I want to wait till the perfect time.

27

Grover

AFTER ONE WEEK home from the hospital, Lindsay's cuts, gashes, and abrasions are healing, but some are still a little red and swollen. She was discharged after three days and was told to follow up with a female doctor.

I've tried talking to her about what happened, and why she had to go see a gynecologist, but she didn't want to talk about it. I know that the doctor had to sow the area where Fernando stabbed her in the upper pelvic region, and it needs to be watched since that's a hard area to keep the suture closed.

Tawney has been by her side since she arrived home. Those two are stuck together like glue. Lindsay's mother has been in an uproar since Calvin, her husband, is back. We still don't know how he found out, but when he got wind that his little girl was hurt, he caught the red-eye flight out and hasn't left her side since the accident.

Cole and I have been working nonstop, filling out paperwork on what went down. Clutch and Bear are being questioned more since they were there when someone shot down all of Fernando's men. The feds are shocked that even after multiple questioning and the polygraph, everything shows we all are on the same page about what happened.

I remember sergeant Filo asking what happened to Fernando. I just shrugged my shoulders and told him he ran after the last gunshot went off. The sergeant knows better, but he doesn't push about it anymore. There is no evidence that proves Fernando is dead or alive.

"Dude, we need to hurry up. Everyone is at the dock, waiting to go fishing." Cole smirks.

"I'm just finishing up now." I place my papers into the manila envelope and hand it to the officer watching me like a hawk.

The sun beams down on my face as I walk towards the truck. The weatherman says today will be a scorcher.

"Damn, bro, we could cook some eggs out here." Cole chuckles, opening the door.

I climb in and crank my beauty up with the air on full blast. I shift the gear into drive and pull off the side of the road. I can't wait to do some fishing. I've got the perfect bait.

I fly into the loading dock, cutting the truck off. We both jump out and start jogging towards the pier where the whole crew awaits.

"Slow your ass down. These flip-flops are tearing in between my toes," Cole bitches from behind me. We changed into some comfortable shoes since we will be standing up for hours, waiting on a bite.

The wooden dock is rocking from the waves from a boat that just zoomed by. I make it to the center console of the boat where Holly stands with her arms crossed. "Damn, guys, I was really close to leaving you." She turns to this tall Asian man behind her and points. "Guys, meet my uncle Osamu; he goes by Big O."

I can't resist the laugh bubbling inside my chest. I bark out this loud chuckle. My shoulders shake as I double over, holding my stomach to catch my breath. "Shit, I'm so sorry."

Holly's uncle leans down and mumbles in my ear, "Shi ni tai-no,"

Well, shit, I don't know their language, but I do know he is probably threatening to kill me. "Sorry, Big O. My brain is a little fried after being interrogated all day."

"Okay, guys. Let's put that ego away and focus on why we are here. Time to get a big-ass fish." Holly claps her hands to bring our attention to her.

She is grinning so big. Big O turns from me, giving Holly a wink then looks back at me with a tight lip. I move around him, heading toward the center where Cole sits talking to the captain.

★ ★ ★

EXCITED ENERGY COURSES through my bouncing knee while I wait for a fish to take a bite of my bait. Several other guys have already got some big carp and barbel. Holly squeals when her line takes off across the water. Her uncle rushes over to help her reel it in. This catfish is huge. They pull it into the boat, and it is longer than my leg.

Suddenly, my line goes down. I grab the rod and jerk up one time to make sure I get it hooked. I start working the reel in closer and closer then walk backwards and quickly reel. A fucking alligator comes floating on top of the water with my hook and the meat swallowed in its mouth.

Everyone comes rushing over. Big O is laughing and talking Japanese. I'm confused about why this is so funny to him. I get the gator close to the boat, and some of Big O's men rope the reptile's mouth.

After about thirty minutes of fighting this huge-ass gator, we get it into the boat. This thing is striking at us with its tail. Cole and several others get the reptile secure and tied up. Big O chuckles, and with the help of two others, they get the gator's mouth open. He reaches in and pulls out the white, wrinkled salami thing out with the hook.

"Holy fuck," I say. "You switched my bait for Fernando's dick to fish with? Oh, hell, no!"

28

Lindsay

I REACH FOR my popcorn on the side table. Tawney put on a movie called Water Boy, with Adam Sandler. I haven't laughed this hard in years. The whole week has been crazy with everyone hovering over me like I'm a little baby. Now it's quiet, and the only people here at my old house are my mom and Tawney.

I was shocked to see my father at the hospital. He saw the news and got the first flight out. He told me he is gifting me the house so mom and I can live there and not be homeless. Mom told him she still wanted a divorce.

Tawney offered to branch out her clothing line and let me be in charge of the ladies' wear.

Things are looking up for me. I have one little secret to tell Grover, and I'm saving that for tonight.

"Honey, are you sure you want to sell this home?" Mom asks, lifting a handful of popcorn and popping it in her mouth.

"Yes, mom, I do. Once I give Grover the news and I know he won't run for the hills, then this house is on the market."

"I think it's a good idea to pack up and move down to the beach with us. Sometimes, leaving bad memories to start good ones is the best thing to do." Tawney throws popcorn at mom.

"You better behave, Tawney. I will have that baby so spoiled you won't know what to do with him or her." She smiles but pops one eyebrow up, teasing her.

These two are too damn funny. I would have never thought I would get this back, being so happy.

After the movie ends, the front door opens and a loud commotion echoes down the foyer.

"The guys are home." Mom scoots out of her chair.

Grover and Cole went fishing with a couple of their buddies this afternoon after their morning briefing at the police station. Fernando went missing, and no one can find him. I'm petrified he will come back to harm us both, but the guys swear to it that he will never be able to come close to any of their loved ones again.

Holly left that day at the hospital, and I haven't heard from her since. She did say she had a lot to get done before heading home with her uncle. I hope she will be okay. I could tell she really didn't want to go back.

Dad is gone back to his new home in Iceland. Why the hell he chose that place, beats me, but since he did commit adultery, their divorce will be final next week. He will fly in for that and luckily won't be back in the states after that.

Sadi is in intensive care for severe dehydration and an infection in her bloodstream that almost killed her. The doctors said she died on them twice in the ER, but now that they found what antibiotic works, she should be good in no time.

Grover walks into the living room, face solid red like a beet. "Damn, baby, you look fine in my pajamas."

Since my clothes are a little tighter and it hurts my cuts, I just wear his baggy clothes. The hungry stare he is giving me sends warm feelings down below. I have been really horny lately, and it doesn't help much that he refuses to touch me until I am healed.

"Come on," he says, breaking my thoughts. I stand up, and Grover wraps his hand around my waist. "Night, everyone. Lindsay and I have some business to handle. See everyone in the morning."

He picks me up and carries me to the bedroom and over to the bed, placing me on the edge. "Let's get these pants off, baby. I sure have missed this pussy." He runs his finger through the top of the elastic band, leans towards me, and nips at my lip.

I groan. I could feel moisture pool between my legs. I can't wait to feel his tongue caressing me. He pulls away and just stares at me. I know he is making sure I'm okay to continue. I had a few nightmares at night. Fernando still haunts me with that blade. I can still feel each sting of the cuts he marked on my skin.

I cup his chin, "Don't ever think your touch reminds me of his. I know guilt eats you up inside that you couldn't protect me from him. I want to forget that painful time and move on to something better. And that's you and our baby." I wait patiently for Grover to catch on to what I just said.

"Holy shit balls! Did you just say what I think you said?" He places his hand on my stomach. "We are having a baby?" He stands up quickly and starts to pace back and forth in front of me. He is mumbling stuff I don't understand. I'm a little nervous at this point.

He picks me up off the bed, my feet dangling above the ground, and I wrap my arms around his neck. He hugs me tightly. "I can't believe this. I'm going to be a father!"

Grover admitting he is happy brings me to tears. "I was so scared of what your reaction would be. I love you." I can finally say the words.

He starts to cry. "I'm scared but happy at the same time. But I do promise you, I will do everything in my power to protect you and my baby. I promise to love you and the baby for the rest of my life."

I trace his lips with my finger, "Oh, babe, I know you will."

He places his hand on my shoulder, "Okay, time to get to business. I've been missing that pussy of yours."

My legs dangle off the bed after he pushes me back. He starts placing kisses down my abdomen and around my navel then dips his tongue inside. His wet tongue swirls around then travels down to my sweet spot and sucks. My hips involuntarily buck from his talented touch. Damn, that sent tingling sensations right to my core. He nibbles his way back up, penetrating me, and I start rocking my hips on his fingers.

"Yes!" I scream while his fingers work their magic against my G-spot. I grab a handful of his hair while I ride my orgasm out.

"Damn, that was intense," I say out of breath.

"It was perfect. Now roll over, baby. Let me fuck you from behind. I want to feel all of you."

I roll over, sticking my ass up in the air. This is my favorite position. He growls, grabbing my hips and easing his dick inside me. The wetness pools more, and he starts to slam into me harder. Our skin slaps against each other. He slaps the cheek of my ass then grips my hip harder, fucking me like a wild animal.

"Fuck yes, baby, that feels so good. I'm about to cum."

I clamp my walls tightly around him, knowing it will drive him wild. He grunts loudly, and hot semen splashes inside me. He collapses to the side, bringing me with him. We are both breathing heavily, holding one another.

A few minutes later, we both get up and head to the bathroom to clean up. We get all washed up and ready to get back in bed when he reaches around with both arms and pulls me against his chest. "I sure do love you, Lindsay. I never pictured my life with someone and especially not with children, but I want to spend the rest of my life with you, fight with you, and give you the proper love a woman deserves. I don't have a ring just yet, but I would love for you to be my wife."

He lets go of me, turning me around to face him. He kneels on one knee, reaches for my hand, and places it directly over his heart. "I give my heart to you. It's all yours. Will you marry me?"

I fall to my knees in front of him and throw my arms around his neck. I crush my lips over his and whisper, "Yes, I will marry you."

He picks me up, twirling me around in circles. He is smiling from ear to ear. I have no idea how life is going to turn out. After losing so much, I thought I would never move on, but then my knight in shining armor comes busting into my life, sweeping me right off my feet. He saved me from destruction, and I showed him what true love could be. We make a perfect couple.

Beach life

W E'VE BEEN ON the beach for two hours. Grover and Cole built this huge sandcastle with water all around it. They decorated it with different seashells. Thaxton, their baby boy, crawled over to it, smushing it like a pancake with his shovel. Tawney and I burst out laughing when the guys fall to the ground, pitching a fit that their hard work is destroyed. Thaxton giggles and smashes the rest of it gleefully.

Grover and I are laying on a blanket while Cole goes to help get the baby's tent fix so Tawney and Thaxton can take a nap.

"How's my little one doing?" Grover talks to my belly.

"She is doing really good. Feels like she is doing somersaults in here."

At that moment, you could see her foot press against my skin. It's amazing how you can see the outline of her little foot. I remember the day we found out it was a girl like it was yesterday.

"Good morning, Mrs. and Mr. Spikes. Are you ready to find out what this little one is?" Dr. Pope asks. He rolls over the machine to the bed.

They've been keeping a good eye on my amniotic fluid. For some reason, it's lower than it should be. Dr. Pope says it could be my elevated blood pressure. He put me on a low dose of hypertension medication. I must drink ten glasses of water a day. I told Grover just to get me a bedpan, so I don't have to get up every thirty minutes to pee.

"All right, let's look at the oligohydramnios fluid to see if it's within normal range then on to the big surprise."

He squirts the cool gel on my stomach, pressing the wand down and moving it around on my belly. A swooshing sound suddenly fills the room then we hear a thumping sound.

The doctor keeps pressing the wand down a little harder and jiggling it a little. Then we see the three little lines. Our little angel. A girl, Dr. Pope tells us. Grover sticks his nose right up to the machine and asks the doctor if he is sure it's a girl. We all laughed.

I entwine my fingers with Grover's as they rest on my stomach. "I can't wait to meet Isabella. Tawney and I made a bet that our kids were going to be boyfriend and girlfriend." I giggle at the face he makes.

His eyebrow goes high, making a crease on his forehead. He has red spots on his neck. "No boys will get my girl. She will always be daddy's little girl. Nope, she is not allowed to have any boyfriends." He shakes his head from side to side.

I open my mouth to speak but then close it. I'm trying to think of how to respond to this. I mean, Isabella will grow up. She will start having crushes. Poor boy that catches her eye.

"Honey, you know she will eventually start getting crushes. Are you going to tell her no?" I ask.

He mumbles something under his breath. "When that time comes, then I will see how I will act, but I don't want to think about that at all. Makes me want to put her in an all-girls school."

I lean over and kiss him on the cheek. "Everything is going to be okay. Watch and see. Thaxton is going to be her protector. You just watch. He'll be like his daddy and uncle."

He grunts.

"Hey, guess what, guys!" Cole comes out of the tent, heading over to us.

"What?" We both ask in unison.

"Clarissa just called, said she needs our help to find her sister."

That's wrong, what my brother and her mother did to her. Even though she went behind Tawney's back and slept with my brother, what Ben did was way worse. When I found out he slept with Clarissa's mother, I was floored. He was just a teenager. Gross. Now Clarissa is a single mother with my nephew, working two jobs, and now she wants to meet her sister, who's also the half-sibling of her child. That is some fucked up shit right there. I attempted to write to Ben, but I think my brother deserves to be in jail. I know it's going to take a lot for Tawney to forgive Clarissa for what she has done, but women always stick together, especially us three.

The End

Made in United States
Orlando, FL
07 January 2025

57026826R00088